MIDDLE SCHOOL

HOW I SURVIVED
BULLIES,
BROCCOLI, AND SNAKE HILL

Also by James Patterson

MIDDLE SCHOOL

HOW I SURVIVED BULLIES, BROCCOLI, AND SNAKE HILL

James Patterson

AND CHRIS TEBBETTS

ILLUSTRATED BY LAURA PARK

HUMONGOUS THANKS TO DR. ELARAJ, DR. HAHR, AND DR. LOCATELLI FOR PATCHING ME UP. ALSO THANKS TO THE VOLUNTEERS AND MEMBERS OF GILDA'S CLUB CHICAGO.
—L.P.

Published by Young Arrow, 2013

2 4 6 8 10 9 7 5 3 1

Copyright © James Patterson, 2013
Illustrations by Laura Park

James Patterson has asserted his right under the Copyright, Designs
and Patents Act 1988 to be identified as the author of this work

First published in Great Britain in 2013 by
Young Arrow
Random House, 20 Vauxhall Bridge Road,
London SW1V 2SA

www.randomhouse.co.uk

Addresses for companies within The Random House Group Limited can be found at:
www.randomhouse.co.uk/offices.htm

The Random House Group Limited Reg. No. 954009

A CIP catalogue record for this book
is available from the British Library

Hardback ISBN 9780099567554
Trade paperback ISBN 9780099567561

The Random House Group Limited supports the Forest Stewardship
Council® (FSC®), the leading international forest-certification organisation.
Our books carrying the FSC label are printed on FSC®-certified paper. FSC is the only
forest-certification scheme supported by the leading environmental organisations,
including Greenpeace. Our paper procurement policy can be found at:
www.randomhouse.co.uk/environment

Printed and bound in Great Britain by Clays Ltd, St Ives Plc

**FOR JACK,
WHO SURViVED LiFE
WiTH SUE AND ME,
AND MADE iT TO
HiGH SCHOOL
—J.P.**

CHAPTER 1

A SLAM-BAM *ENDiNG*?!

Do you ever read the first line of a book and SLAM the thing shut? I sure do.

I hope you didn't do that to my story. Guess I'll never know.

Anyway, hi. I'm Rafe Khatchadorian, and if you already know me, then you know I do things a little differently than most people. I like to break the rules. No, I *love* to break rules. Especially dumb ones, like no talking in the hallways at my school and only being allowed to use the bathroom two times a day, no matter what.

So I don't know if this has been done before in the history of books, but I'm going to tell you some of the ways this story might end. And I'm going to do it right here at the *beginning* of the book.

I went to summer camp/summer school this year. But before the full eight weeks were up, things went kind of cuckoo-crazy (okay, a *lot* cuckoo-crazy), and I ended up packing my bags early. (Actually, some camp counselors packed them for me.)

My unexpected departure might have had something to do with this emergency situation:

Or maybe what happened was more like this unfortunate event:

It also could have gone something like this:

Or like this picture, which says about ten thousand words:

I can tell you for sure that it had something to do with this little disaster:

Somewhere in all of that, there's an ending to this crazy story. There's some middle in there too.

But that's as much as I'm going to tell you for now. If you want all the gory details, you're going to have to read on. At your own risk.

I'll tell you this much: This is a tale of bullies and broccoli, of shocking bravery and even more shocking cowardliness (or however you say that), of gallons of puke, of friends and fiends, and of being totally, hopelessly lost on a place called Snake Hill.

I promise: You won't be bored.

Maybe you read *Middle School, The Worst Years of My Life*. Well, this was the Worst Summer of My Life.

But it was also—weirdly—the best.

CHAPTER 2

WELCOME TO CAMP WANNAMORRA

Now that we've gotten the ending out of the way, I guess we can start the story.

You know those regular-type camps, where kids with spiffy haircuts spend the summer running around in the fresh air, and roasting marshmallows to an even brown, and swimming in the lake all day long? Maybe you've even been to one of those places.

HUFF
HUFF

Role Model Camp Kid

Well, hold that thought. Here's another question:

Have you ever read that book *Holes*? If you haven't, you should, because it's an awesome book. But there was a camp in that story too—Camp

Read this book, but finish my story first, okay?

Green Lake, which was actually a prison for kids.

Let's say that the place I went, Camp Wannamorra, was somewhere right in the middle of all that. Half camp and half prison. And by "prison" I mean *school*.

That's right. Me. Summer school. AGAIN.

Every morning from eight to twelve at Camp Wannamorra, we were going to be in classes. I was going to take the kind for kids who need a little extra help. And my brainiac sister, Georgia, was going to take the "Challenge Program," for kids who had nothing better to do on vacation than get smarter than they already were. It didn't sound anything like camp to me.

The more Mom talked about it, the more excited Georgia got, which made me even more suspicious. Mom kept calling it "summer camp," but I was pretty sure it was going to look something like this.

If you read my last two books—or even my sister Georgia's stupid story—then you know that *school* isn't exactly my best subject. I've already "done time" at Hills Village Middle School and Cathedral School of the Arts *and* Airbrook Arts. (I'm kind of, sort of, an artist, but more about that later.)

The bottom line was, if I wanted to keep going to Airbrook, I needed to "do some remedial work" over the summer.

CHAPTER 3

GOOD-BYE AND GOOD LUCK (BECAUSE, RAFE, YOU'RE GOING TO NEED IT)

My mom and Grandma Dotty drove me and Georgia up to camp for the first day.

"You sure you have everything we packed? Everything you need?" Mom asked us about ten times from the front seat of our smoking—and I mean smoking in a *bad* way—eighteen-year-old family van.

"I'm sure!" Georgia said. "And in fact, I'm sure that I'm sure."

Georgia had packed about eight weeks in advance, checked her list forty times, and then made a copy of the list to make sure she wouldn't lose it...and double-checked that too. My sister may be smart, but she's also nuttier than a squirrel's nest on the first day of winter.

"Rafe, what about you?" Mom asked, because I'm kind of the opposite of Georgia. "Do you have everything you need?"

"Um…I guess so," I said. "Y'know, like I said last time you asked. Three minutes ago."

The good news was that we had a whole lake between the boys' side of the camp and the girls' side. If I was lucky, I'd hardly see Georgia at all for the whole eight weeks. It almost made the summer-school thing worth it. (I said *almost*.)

When we drove onto the camp grounds, we got to the boys' side first. I pulled out my stuff from the back and tried to make a clean getaway, but Mom's pretty mushy about this stuff. She needed to get in a few hugs before I could go.

"I know it's school, but it's camp too," she said. "I think you just might have a good time. I really do!"

"Assuming you don't get eaten by a bear," Grandma said. She was looking at the camp brochure. "Or lost on Snake Hill. Or—"

"Snake Hill?" Georgia said from the backseat. "There's a Snake Hill here? What does that mean? Like... real snakes? Really?"

I love Grandma Dotty, but sometimes she says stuff without thinking about it. "So long, kiddo!" she said. She reached over then and hugged me too, really tight, the way she always does. "You're either going to love it, or you're going to hate it here. Put that in your pipe and smoke it." (My grandma says stuff like that all the time.)

Anyway, I was kind of nervous. It's one thing to be a nobody at school, when you can go home at the end of the day. It's another thing to get dropped off in the middle of the woods, with a camp full of total strangers who you're going to be living with, eating with, and sleeping with for the next fifty-six days and nights (or so I thought at the time).

"Come on, Jules," Grandma said. "Camp doesn't start until the parents leave. We need to drop off Miss Georgia and skedaddle!"

"Georgia? Rafe?" Mom said. "Do you want to say good-bye to each other?"

"Not really," Georgia said.

"Whatever," I said.

"Well, do it anyway," Mom said.

Okay, one more little bit of truth here. It was true that I couldn't wait to get away from Georgia, even if we would just be on two sides of the same camp. But now that Mom and Grandma were about to take off, some teeny, tiny part of me was glad that Georgia would be around. I don't know why. I just was.

And for the record, if you ever tell her I said that, I'm going to hunt you down and put fire ants in your sleeping bag.

You've been warned.

CHAPTER 4

MEET THE BOOGER EATER

I guess that the first day of camp is a little like the first day of school. You can spot the popular kids right away, because they've already latched on to a giant blob of about a million friends. Other kids just look kind of lost. (Guess which group I was in?)

So far, it was all too familiar.

When I gave my name to the nearest counselor with a clipboard, he looked at his list and said, "Yep, here you are. Rafe Khatchadorian. You'll be with Rusty and the Muskrats."

I had no idea what that meant. It sounded like some kind of terrifyingly bad band.

"Just take your gear and head down that path," he said. He pointed into the woods. "It's the fifth cabin on your right."

From the parking lot, I followed the twisty path he showed me and counted the other cabins along the way. The first one had a sign on the front that said ANT HILL and a bunch of little kids running around in front. After that came Sly Fox Run, then Bald Eagle's Nest, then Grizzly Bear Cave, and finally. . . Muskrat Hut.

And I thought—*seriously*? I could have been an Eagle or a Bear or a Fox, but no. For the next eight weeks, I was going to be a Muskrat. Great.

The first person I met was Rusty, our cabin counselor. He was waiting, right there on the front porch steps, with his own clipboard.

Cabin counselor is kind of like homeroom teacher—except Rusty wasn't like any homeroom teacher I'd ever seen before. He was more like three teachers, all packed into one body. And I don't mean that he was fat. He looked like the kind of guy who spent all day at the gym and then dreamed about lifting weights at night just so he could get in an extra workout. Even his muscles had muscles.

"Hey, Rafe, dude, super cool to meet you!" he said, while he broke most of the bones in my hand. "You pumped? I hope you're pumped, 'cause we're going to have a super-awesome time this summer."

"Um…awesome?" I said, because I didn't know what else to say.

Meanwhile, there was a whole bunch of insane yelling and pounding coming from inside the cabin. It sounded like my cabinmates were tearing it down from the inside out, but Rusty didn't seem to care or even notice. The only other person I could actually see was this skinny kid on the front porch, reading the thickest book I've ever seen.

"Yo, Norman!" Rusty said. "Put down the

Encyclopedia Normanica a sec and come meet your bunk mate."

I'm not going to lie. All I thought when I saw him was, *I hope this kid brought sunblock.* He looked like he'd just crawled out from under some rock.

And then I thought, *Wow.* His glasses were about as thick as his book. It didn't take a genius to guess that he was here for the Challenge Program, not for the one for kids like me.

"Rafe, Norman. Norman, Rafe," Rusty said. When we shook hands, it was a little like grabbing hold of an uncooked chicken cutlet. "Why don't you show him where he's bunking?"

"Sure," Norman said, pulling open the squeaky, old screen door to the cabin. "And thanks, Rusty."

"For what?" he said.

"For not calling me—"

"BOOGER EATER!" came a chorus of voices from inside the cabin.

Then a pillow flew out the door and practically knocked Norman off the porch. Not that it would take that much. I kind of felt sorry for him right away.

Except then I started thinking...

On the inside, the cabin was pretty basic. And by basic, I mean that cavemen would have asked for an upgrade. On the windows, there were just screens with holes and rips, no glass, and four seriously lopsided bunk beds. You could see between the floorboards to the ground outside, and the ceiling was just big wooden beams, all the way up to the roof. That's where most of the other guys were, crawling around. And that's where the next two pillows came from.

"BOOGER EATER!"

"NEW KID!"

One of the flying pillows caught me in the face. The other one whizzed past Norman. He acted like it hadn't even happened.

"This is your bunk," he said. It was a bottom one, and closest to the door. All the other beds were taken. I guess that's what you get for being the last one in. Not only was I bunking with a kid named Booger Eater, but if we got visited by a grizzly bear in the middle of the night, guess who was first in line on the all-you-can-eat human buffet?

Still, I was going to worry about that later. For now, I was trying to figure out if these guys were piling on because I was the new kid or because I was already part of the group. Or both. They seemed kind of okay, though.

What I did know was that as long as Norman the Booger Eater was around, I had an above-average shot at not being the biggest loser in the cabin. That was worth something, right?

The Muskrats. The Muskrats? The Muskrats! (It doesn't matter how you say it—it still sounds lame.)

Here, let me introduce you to the guys.

CHAPTER 5

~~WHO'S~~ WHAT'S FOR DINNER?

You know what, Nuke?" Dweebs told me. "You're going to fit right in here."

Say what?

"Nuke?" I said.

Dweebs just kind of shrugged. "It's short for New Kid. You're the only one who wasn't here last year."

I guess everyone at Camp Wannamorra had a nickname. Or at least all the Muskrats did. Besides, I didn't mind Nuke so much. It was better than some of the other possibilities. Like Booger Eater.

Meanwhile, all that moving in had worked up an appetite, I guess. By the time they rang the big dinner bell down at the main building, I was starving.

"Don't get too excited," Smurf told me. "Not unless you're a big fan of mushy oatmeal."

"Or mushy broccoli," Cav said.

"Yeah," Two Tunz said. "I lost ten pounds last summer. And that was *after* the pie-eating contest."

I didn't even care, though. At least I wouldn't be eating alone. Camp had only started an hour ago, and I already had a cabin full of friends.

We all walked down to the Chow Pit together. Cav told me that was the name for the cafeteria. But when we got there, I didn't see a cafeteria at all. Just a bunch of rickety picnic tables in a big circle on the grass, with a little hut off to the side.

"This is it?" I said. "There's not even a roof. What if it gets hot out?"

"Then we sweat," Bombardier told me.

"What if it rains?" I asked.

"Then the meat loaf isn't so dry," Two Tunz said with a laugh. He and Bombardier high-fived right over my head.

Every cabin had its own picnic table in the circle. We sat down at the Muskrat table while Rusty went with the other counselors to get the plates and silverware and stuff. That left about a hundred campers outside, all running around and laughing and talking at once.

At first, I didn't really notice anything out of the ordinary. It was just a bunch of blah-blah-blah and buzz-buzz-buzz all around me.

But then...I started to hear stuff I didn't like.

I was just starting to put two and two together, when I heard someone from a couple tables over who was louder than everyone else.

"What's for dinner?" the voice asked.

"Dead meat!" someone else said.

"What's for dinner?" the voice asked again.

This time, a bunch of guys answered and pounded on the table at the same time. "DEAD! MEAT!"

"Oh, man," Smurf said. "Here we go."

When I looked over, I saw the kid who was leading the whole thing, and I knew his type right away. Put it this way: If you took the words *cocky* and *conceited* and *pain in the butt* and then combined them all into one big word...and then looked *that* word up in the dictionary, you'd see a picture of this guy.

"Who's that?" I said.

"Doolin," Smurf told me. "He's in the Bobcat cabin. Just ignore him."

But I didn't really see how. Every time Doolin said "What's for dinner?" and every time the other Bobcats answered "Dead meat!" they were all looking right at us. *We* were the dead meat.

The other guys at my table were just shaking their heads or looking at the ground, except for Norman, who was reading, and Legend, who was... *laughing*? I had no idea what Legend's deal was, but he obviously thought this was pretty funny.

I only *wished* I thought it was funny.

"What's for dinner?" Doolin kept going, like a Britney Spears song that repeats over and over and over till you want to yank your ears right off your head.

"DEAD! MEAT!"

"What's for—"

Then somebody else yelled out even louder. "Yo! Doolin!" I looked over, and Rusty was standing there. "Have a seat, dude."

"What? I'm just playin' around," he said.

"I know, man. But have a seat anyway."

"What-ev," Doolin said, and high-fived the kid next to him before he took his time sitting down.

I was glad Rusty was back. But then again, this was only the first day. Something told me Rusty wasn't always going to be there, and that Doolin and his wrecking crew weren't done with us.

That wasn't all either.

So far, I'd been feeling like I'd lucked out, getting into this crazy, cool cabin of guys. But now I was starting to think maybe all of us Muskrats had something in common with Booger Eater, and I hadn't realized it. Maybe we were the biggest losers at Camp Wannamorra.

And maybe everyone already knew it.

CHAPTER 6

I DON'T CARE ABOUT YOUR STINKING RULES!

Once we'd finished eating the mystery meat, mystery veg, and mystery dessert (that might have also been meat, I'm not sure), it was time for after-dinner announcements. This old guy I didn't recognize got up in the middle of the Chow Pit and clapped his hands for everyone to be quiet. Amazingly, everything got real quiet, real fast.

"Who's that?" I asked Dweebs.

"That's Major Sherwood," he said. "We call him the

Dictator. You definitely don't want to get on his bad side. And he doesn't *have* a good side."

"Really?" I said. "He looks kind of harmless."

"I know, right?" Smurf said. "Go figure."

"Hello, boys!" Major Sherwood said. "And welcome to another summer at Camp Wannamorra!"

Everyone clapped and cheered then, including me, since I didn't know any better.

"This is the first and last time your counselors will be waiting on you, so don't get used to it," Sherwood said, all smiley-faced. "The young men of Camp Wannamorra look out for themselves. Isn't that right, boys?"

"Yes, sir!" a bunch of the campers yelled back. This time, I noticed that nobody at my table said a word, except for Rusty.

After that, things started sounding a little more...familiar.

"As most of you know, I like to run a tight ship around here," Sherwood said. "To that end, there are certain guidelines one needs to follow. So let's start off by going over a few of the expectations we have of our campers here, shall we?"

It was all getting clearer by the second. Tight

ship? Guidelines? Expectations? Just another way of saying RULES, RULES, and MORE RULES.

And Camp Wannamorra had plenty of them. I know, because Major Sherwood told us about every single one.

There were rules about not wasting water or electricity or food or paper or "other resources" (whatever that meant).

There were rules about keeping our cabins clean every day and about taking a shower at least once a week.

Camp Wannamorra was a "Personal Electronics–Free Zone," which meant that anyone caught with a phone or an iPod or a laptop could kiss it good-bye for the rest of the summer.

We weren't allowed to wander off by ourselves, and we definitely weren't allowed to go into the adults-only areas of the camp.

Curfew was nine o'clock. Sharp. No exceptions.

Lights-out was ten o'clock. Sharp. No exceptions.

Wake-up was seven o'clock. Sharp. Unless you were up at six or five.

School started at eight (sharp, like a needle to the eye).

There was absolutely no storing of food in the cabins. No sneaking over to the girls' camp. No this, no that, no…I'm not even sure what else. My brain hit FULL a long time before Major Sherwood was anywhere near done. But I was definitely starting to see where his nickname came from.

Finally, somewhere after dinner and before the end of time, I guess that Major Sherwood ran out of rules to tell us about.

"All righty, then," he said. "Enough of that. How about we have a little fun before curfew?"

That sounded good to me. I was hoping he meant Capture the Flag, or making s'mores, or something like that. But instead, someone handed him a guitar, and he started playing. And you know what? He was even worse than my sister, Georgia, who plays in a band called We Stink.

I actually recognized the tune of the song. It was this old one Mom used to sing in the car. She said it was called "Guantanamera," which is Spanish for something, but I always thought it sounded like "One-Ton Tomato."

It turned out that "One-Ton Tomato" was also the camp song, but with its own words.

Camp Wan-na-morra!
We're here at Camp Wan-na-morra!
Camp Wan-na-moooooooor-ra!
We all love Camp Wan-na-morra!

Everyone sang along off-key while Major Sherwood played his guitar and walked around from table to table. And even though I was still learning the new words, I moved my mouth up and down and pretended like I was singing. It was only the first night of camp, after all. I didn't know what Dweebs meant about not getting on Sherwood's bad side, but I figured this wasn't the time to find out.

Hopefully, if the real fun ever started, somebody would let me know.

We're here at Camp Wan-na-morra!
Eight weeks at Camp Wan-na-morra!
Please help me get through to-morr-a.

CHAPTER 7

LOSERVILLE

After a couple more oldy-but-moldy songs like "On Top of Spaghetti" and "B-I-N-G-O" and "Help Me, Help Me, Someone Please Get Me Out of This Crazy Camp That's Really Just a School with a Lake" (okay…two out of three, anyway), Major Sherwood finally, mercifully, let us go for the night.

All of us Muskrats walked back to our cabin together, joking around and acting like that whole "dead meat" thing never happened. Or maybe it was just me. Maybe nobody else was even thinking about it anymore. They all seemed pretty okay—

At least until we got to the Muskrat Hut.

That's when we saw the sign someone had made. It was on a giant piece of paper taped over the screen door. In big black letters, it said WELCOME TO LOSERVILLE.

Oh, man. I'm not saying I knew for a *fact* that Doolin and the other Bobcats were behind this. But it seemed like a no-brainer to me. It was obviously them.

The guys just stood there in front of the cabin. Nobody said anything for a second.

But guess what? A second is all the time I need.

In fact, it's more than enough time—for *Nuke Khatchadorian*.

I take off at nuclear speed and head straight for Doolin's cabin. As I approach, I can sense him through the walls, and no, I don't bother with the door. I bust right through the spot in the wall where he's sitting on his bunk. By the time anyone even notices he's gone, there's just an empty bed and a Rafe-shaped hole left behind.

Quicker than light, I swing past the lake, with Doolin hanging upside down.

Please don't drop me, Mr. Khatchadorian!

I dip him in just enough to get his head wet and keep going. Next thing you know, I'm back at the Muskrat Hut. I fly back and forth, back and forth, faster than the human eye can see, using Doolin's head like a scrub brush to wipe that Loserville sign out of existence. If he's a little bald by tomorrow... well, that's not my problem.

Finally, as that second on the clock pushes into the home stretch, so do I.

I whip Doolin back to where he started, drop him on his bunk, and fly back to my own guys, who are standing there looking at the place where that sign used to be.

And...*TICK!*

What just happened to me?

"Did you guys see something?" Dweebs says. "Like a...sign or something?"

"Uh...I kind of thought so," Smurf says, scratching his blue head. "But I guess not."

"Must have been an illusion," I say.

After that, everyone goes inside, nobody even knows that stupid sign was ever there in the first place, and our summer at Camp Wannamorra starts to look a whole lot brighter.

Yeah...

Yeah...

Yeah...I wish.

Thanks, guys, I couldn't have done it without you!

CHAPTER 8

PUT A LIGHT ON THE SUBJECT

poiler alert! I wish I could say that the rest of the night went okay, but it didn't.

After lights-out, Rusty went off to the counselors' dorm, which I guess is like the teachers' lounge, if the teachers slept at school. Supposedly, they had real food in the dorm, and some of the counselors from the girls' side came over to hang out at night and I don't know what else. (That kind of stuff, as teachers say, isn't exactly "age appropriate.")

A little after that, before any of us were asleep, I heard footsteps outside. There was whispering. And snickering too.

Then a flashlight came on—right through the

window and right in my face, so I couldn't see a
thing.

"What time is it?" someone whispered.

"Dead meat!" someone else said.

"Wha...?" I said. "That doesn't even make sense."

Then another light came on—this time it was
shining in Cav's face, on his bunk.

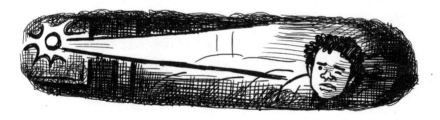

"What time is it?" another voice said.

"Dead meat!" they all whispered.

"Buzz off!" Cav yelled at them then, but they
just laughed some more.

Then a third light came on. I saw it across the
cabin. It was coming right into the window next to
Legend's top bunk. Except when
it came on, he was
already waiting
for it.

"What time is—"

"YOU JUST PICKED THE WRONG INMATE
TO MESS WITH!" Legend said. "I'M TALKING TO
YOU, DOOLIN. YOU HEAR ME? BAD CHOICE...
VERY BAD CHOICE!"

Okay, I've got a couple of things to say about all that. In fact, here's everything I was thinking while Doolin and the other Bobcats went running for the hills:

1. That was the first time I'd ever heard Legend speak.
2. Sweet! It looked like the Muskrats might have a secret weapon.
3. Unless…maybe he wasn't *our* secret weapon at all. Maybe he was more like a nightmare living in the same room as we were.
4. In which case…what, exactly, was this kid capable of? What had he done in the past that the Bobcats were so scared of now?
5. Did *I* need to be scared of him?
6. Hmmm…

CHAPTER 9

WiDE AWAKE!

Was Legend sleeping? I sure wasn't. I was too busy thinking.

Now, the following is way too deep for me to understand—but my old English teacher, Ms. Donatello, once said I have the ability to go from denial to acceptance, and that it's a gift. (Maybe your mom can explain that one to you—or maybe one of your teachers can. I sure can't.)

The point is, I was now certain that very bad things were in store for me and my friends at good old Camp Wannamorra. I accepted that fact.

So I just lay there in bed for a while, staring at the ceiling, wondering what to do about it. Well, I was actually staring at the bottom of Booger Eater's mattress in the dark. Assuming Norman got his nickname for a reason, I could only hope he was more of an Eater than a Flicker. I'm no scientist, but even I know what gravity will do to something that gets flicked off a top bunk, with me down there on the bottom.

Finally, I couldn't stand all this thinking any-more. I grabbed my flashlight, got up, and went outside to the bathroom.

At Camp Wannamorra, the bathroom was called the latrine. This one was more like a concrete bunker, with showers, toilets, and sinks. You had to walk through the woods to get there, which was a whole new thing for me.

And I don't mean I had to *use* the bathroom. I just wanted to *go* there. I've always had pretty good luck getting privacy in bathrooms.

It was also the first chance I had to really talk to Leo.

If you know me, then you've been wondering where old Leo's been all this time. And if you asked my mother that question, she'd say something corny but true. She'd point at my chest, where my heart is, and say that Leo is always there with me.

But if you're sitting there thinking *What the*

heck is this guy talking about, and who is this Leo person? then I should catch you up.

Let's see, how do I say this without sounding too weird? Leo was my twin brother, my absolute best friend when we were little. He got sick and ended up dying. After that, I always wondered what it would be like if he were still around, and it just kept going from there. That's why I have conversations with Leo all the time, inside my head.

Okay, never mind. There's no way to tell you that without it sounding weird.

For the record—I'm not embarrassed about Leo. I still think of him as my friend, besides also being my brother who died. But when you're at a summer camp, and you're living with seven other guys every minute of the day, there's not a whole lot of room for conversations with people who aren't actually there.

And that's what I wanted to talk to Leo about.

"Sorry I haven't been around much," I told Leo.

"It's all right," Leo said. "But we need to talk about this jerk Doolin. What are we going to do about him?"

"That's the thing, Leo," I said. "I've been thinking maybe I need to start figuring out some of this stuff on my own."

"What for?" Leo said. "I've already got a couple of awesome ideas."

Leo always has good ideas. In fact, once he gets started, it's hard to get him to stop. It's not like he needs sleep or anything.

"It's just…I don't think the guys in my cabin would understand," I said.

"Uh-huh," Leo said. "You're probably right. Not everybody can understand about us."

"Don't be mad," I told him.

"I'm not mad."

He was mad.

"I just need to keep all this stuff dialed down for a little while," I said. "It's only eight weeks."

"Yeah, yeah, okay, fine. I get it," Leo said. "Good luck with all that."

That's the other thing about Leo. He's kind of touchy. But I was going to have to worry about that later. I already had enough on my plate to deal with.

Real stuff first.

Sorry, Leo.

CHAPTER 10

ONE CAMP WANNAMORRA MYSTERY SOLVED

WARNING: This is one of the grossest chapters in the book. Not *the* grossest, but probably in the top ten. If you're eating something, you might want to put it down for a second.

So…it felt like I was asleep for about five minutes that night— before they started playing the wake-up song over the camp loudspeaker.

That was seven o'clock. At seven thirty, we had to be at breakfast. That meant

half an hour to get up, get dressed, and do whatever else you had to do in the morning.

Which brings me to how I found out where Bombardier's nickname came from. You might think
about skipping to the next chapter now.

I guess not, huh? Okay, here goes.

After I got dressed, I went back to the latrine before I headed down to the Chow Pit. It was crowded
now, with guys brushing their teeth and doing
whatever—gargling, running their hands through
their crew cuts, Q-tipping their ears and noses.
There I was, waiting my turn, looking around, and
just starting to wonder why I didn't see any of the
other Muskrats, when out of nowhere...

It happened. Now I understand.

It starts with the smell—and it hits you like a
Mack truck up the nose. But it doesn't stop there.
The next thing you know, you're gagging—a little
at first, but if you're not careful, it turns into a full-
on, blown-chunks kind of situation.

That's only if you stick around. Nobody ever does.
Not when Bombardier's been in the latrine. (It goes
like this: Bombardier + broccoli = BOOM!) The only
trick at that point is not getting crushed by the
stampede.

The bad news? Well, just look at the picture.

The good news? I wasn't sure how it might work yet, but maybe the Muskrats had another secret weapon on our hands. Or maybe a *not-so-secret* weapon.

More bad news? I mean, come on! Did you look at the picture?

More good news? Actually, yes: This isn't a scratch-and-sniff book.

CHAPTER 11

SUMMERTIME BLUES... SORT OF

Okay, so it had to happen sometime.

That morning at eight, to be exact.

The start of summer school!

I don't know how much you need to hear about this. You've been to school. You've taken English and social studies and math and all that stuff. The only real difference was that this school was held in a couple of tents on the camp grounds, with signs on them that said THE FUN STARTS HERE!

I was starting to figure out that the people at Camp Wannamorra had a whole different definition of *fun* than I did.

One surprise was that the girls came over for school in the morning too. I even saw Georgia, but we just kind of waved at each other and kept moving. It's not like we were in the same classes or anything.

My group included me, Dweebs, Smurf, and Booger Eater, which was another big surprise.

"I kind of thought you'd be in with the brain patrol," I said. But Booger Eater shrugged it off.

"My mom thinks I could use some extra help," he said.

Still, it seemed weird. He just looked smart. Not to mention that he always had some kind of book surgically attached to his arm. It was hard to imagine a kid like that *not* being good at school.

First period was science. The Challenge Program kids went off to study the lake or something while my group sat in a tent and learned about the human circulatory system...just like I'd learned about it (kind of) at Hills Village Middle School.

Second period was English. Mostly, the teacher talked about the play we were going to put on that summer, *You're a Good Man, Charlie Brown.* I didn't know what that had to do with English, but I guess it could have been worse.

Third period was social studies. (Are you getting bored yet?)

I was just starting to wonder if that morning was ever going to end, when I walked into fourth-period math. That's when I saw our math teacher for the first time.

"Hi, everyone," she said. "I'm Katie Kim. Nice to meet you all."

Her name was Katie Kim.

Katie Kim.

Did I already say Katie Kim? I just wanted to make sure that you knew her name. It was Katie Kim.

Listen, I don't know what love is supposed to feel like, but I definitely had *something* at first sight that morning. She even made me forget about math for a little while.

Actually, scratch that. It doesn't take anything for me to forget about math. But Katie Kim made me just a little bit glad I was there.

I'm not going to say she was the best teacher in the world, because to tell you the truth, I don't really know. I mean, I heard all the words coming out of her mouth, but I wasn't really putting them together into sentences. I was just sitting there, thinking about how much I wished Katie Kim wouldn't ever stop talking.

I mean, it's not like I thought something was going to happen. No way, no how. She was at least in college, and I was…me. But still, I've never felt that way about a teacher, ever, ever, ever—unless Jeanne Galletta counted. She was my tutor back in Hills Village, but that wasn't the same.

Nobody was the same as Katie Kim.

Katie Kim. That was her name. Did I already mention that? Is this getting a little stupid? I don't care. It was still great!

CHAPTER 12

FISHY

Don't get me wrong—I'm not saying it's Katie Kim's fault that I needed extra help with the first math assignment. Not exactly.

But I am saying that if she hadn't been so interesting to look at, I might have known what to do when she started passing out these *Fun with Fractions* workbooks near the end of the period.

When I looked inside, it was kind of familiar, since I'd learned this stuff before, at Hills Village Middle School. But when it comes to school stuff, my brain's like a pocket with a big hole in the bottom.

Besides, what was I going to ask her? *Could you please repeat everything you just said for the last half hour?* I don't think so.

Also, I know from personal experience that I'll do at least one stupid thing every time I try to talk to a pretty girl. (Or woman? Was Katie a woman? I didn't even know.)

Talking to Anyone Else

Talking to Katie

So I asked the guys for help instead. But Dweebs just said, "Uh, I was kind of hoping you could explain it to me," and Smurf was more like, "Well, you know, you just…like…multiply that stuff, like…fractions, you know?"

And then I remembered why we were all in summer school to begin with.

That's when Norman spoke up. He'd been sitting off to the side, minding his own business like always. "It's not that hard," he said. "Just multiply the top numbers together and then the bottom numbers together. Then you reduce the fraction, like this."

He showed me his page. Most of it made sense, except the reducing part, which I never get. But now Norman had me thinking about something else.

"Are you *sure* you're in the right group?" I said. Between the math skills and the reading twenty-eight hours a day, I just wasn't buying it.

"Definitely," he said right away. "I guess math is kind of the exception for me. I'm really bad at everything else."

"Like reading?" I said, but Norman didn't answer. Then before I could ask any more, Katie said the period was over, and Norman got out of there like a hairless cat at a German shepherd convention.

"You know what?" I said to Dweebs and Smurf. "I think that kid's hiding something."

"Nah," Smurf said. "That's just Booger Eater."

But I wasn't so sure. Brains-wise, it seemed obvious to me that Norman the Booger Eater was more of a Georgia Khatchadorian than a Rafe Khatchadorian, if you know what I mean.

Maybe I didn't know how to reduce fractions yet, but I did know one thing for sure: Norman was pretty bad at playing dumb.

The question was—why would he want to?

CHAPTER 13

DROP EVERYTHING AND READ

So imagine this: You've got these four pieces of a dog-poo sandwich that you're supposed to eat. Don't ask me why. (And don't worry, it's not real!) They're just sitting there on a plate in front of you, and you're not going to be allowed to get up until you've eaten every bite.

Okay, now imagine that someone comes along and puts one more piece on your plate.

That's basically what happened after math. Just when I thought it was the end of the school day, I found out we had one more period to go. (Like I said, poo sandwich!)

It turned out that Major Sherwood was all gung ho about reading, just like Norman. So every morning from eleven o'clock to eleven forty-five, everyone at camp, including the teachers, had to sit and do nothing but stare at a book. They called it D.E.A.R., which stands for Drop Everything and Read. Maybe you even have it at your school, but I'd never heard of it.

The only kind of book I'd brought to camp was my sketchbook. I like drawing more than anything, and all that heavy reading was the kind of stuff "good" kids did, like Norman and my sister, Georgia, and Jeanne Galletta back home. Not me.

I mean, don't get me wrong. I'm not *against* books. Heck, you're reading my story right now, and I'm all for that. It's just that, up until now, the only reading I did every day was on the back of cereal boxes.

Still, Major Sherwood was ready for kids like me. After fourth period, he got on the camp loud-speaker and said that anyone who didn't already have a book to read should come down to the library in the main building and pick something out. "NOW!"

Yeah, that's right. Camp Wannamorra had its own library, which is kind of like putting a dentist's office in an amusement park.

Still, the word on the street was—don't cross the Dictator! So I got myself down to the main building right away. I even had a new idea about what to do by the time I got there.

The camp library didn't look much like the libraries I'd seen before. There was no computer, no librarian, not even a scared-looking kid hiding from the bullies in the back.

It was just a big room with a bunch of book-shelves.

I kind of hung back while everyone else started grabbing stuff. Cav took something called *Hatchet*, which I thought might be about serial killers, but it wasn't. And Smurf picked out *The Chocolate War* (which doesn't have a single thing to do with food fights, in case you're wondering).

Then I felt this hand on my shoulder.

"What's your pleasure, Mr. Whatchamacallit?" Major Sherwood asked. It was like the Dictator had come out of nowhere.

"It's Khatchadorian, sir," I said. Nobody ever gets my name right.

"That's what I said," he told me. "Whatchamacallit."

Mom says I need to learn how to choose my battles, so I didn't push it.

"Do you have any of those big books about art?" I asked him.

"Ah! An art lover, are we?" he said.

"Uh…I guess we are."

I knew that a lot of those art books were huge, and that's what I wanted—something really big. Sherwood took me around the corner and showed me a shelf with extra-large books sitting on their sides.

There were books about Russia and world records and dogs, alligators, ladies' jewelry, and a whole bunch of other things. I found two art books. One was on Michelangelo, and the other was about some jumpy guy named Hopper. I took the Michelangelo.

"Good choice," the major said. "Now go find a quiet spot and get to it!"

"Yes, sir," I said.

I went outside and scoped out a tree to lean against so no one could sneak up behind me. Then I opened the Michelangelo book, put my sketchbook inside, and "got to it," like the Dictator had said.

So while everyone else was Dropping Everything and Reading, I was doing what I do best—Dropping Everything and Drawing.

Which I guess made them D.E.A.R. And me D.E.A.D.

CHAPTER 14

GOING FOR
BROWNIE POINTS

P.S. Don't get me wrong about the whole reading thing. I just want to state for the record...

To all schools, parents, and other important people of the world: Please make sure the kids in your life D.E.A.R. every day. (Drop Everything And Read) You'll be glad you did! Even if I don't. I mean, who am I to give advice? Signed, **R.K.** (Which stands for Reading King!) (or not)

CHAPTER 15

PESTILENCE(S)

Question: What's red, bumpy, even uglier than usual, and itches all over?

Answer: Me, after a week at Camp Wannamorra.

Here's something they don't tell you in the camp brochure, just so you know: It's not really Major Sherwood who runs that place. It's not the counselors or even the campers. It's the BUGS.

I'm not even joking. Up in the mountains, they call the mosquitoes "Franken-skeeters." I swear they look like they escaped from some kind of mad scientist's lab. The wasps are as big as birds and have definite anger-management issues. And the no-see-ums are the worst. They're called that because they're so tiny, you can't even *see um*—but you definitely *feel um* once they start chowing

down on you. I think I spent half of that first week
at camp scratching.

And that's just the bugs. I also had Doolin and
his fiends to deal with, not to mention enough
math, science, social studies, and English to choke
a very smart kid going to some great college I don't
even know the name of.

Then there were the counselors. In the brochure,
they all look like movie stars who want to be your
best friend. And to be fair, some of them (Katie,
Katie, Katie) were okay.

Rusty is okay, even if he's kind of clueless. I

call him Wannabe Thor, but not to his face. (You saw those muscles, right?) He also has two best counselor friends, Pete (Wannabe Tony Hawk) and Gordon (Wannabe Donald Trump—including the hair!).

The thing you need to know about the counselors is that they have this favorite "game" they like to play called Kamikaze. And when I say "game," I really mean "form of torture."

It goes like this: Anytime a counselor shouts out "KAMIKAZE!" every camper in sight has to hit the dirt. No matter what. It doesn't matter if you're brushing your teeth, about to catch a fly ball, or spreading manure in a field full of stinkbugs. If you hear that word, you go down. There's no choice.

I mean, you do have a choice, but believe me… you don't have a choice. I saw a kid move too slow on the second day, and he ended up getting wedgied within an inch of his life.

And that's just one of the possibilities. Believe me, the counselors have it down to a science.

WEDGIE (Both traditional and atomic)

More painful if hung off something like a doorknob or branch

Cut me down!

THE DREADED SWIRLIE

Place head here and flush

Don't bother screaming. In fact, keep your mouth closed.

PANTSING Extra points if it happens in front of a large audience. Extra-extra points if it's in front of the girls.

HA   HA HA HA HA HA   HA

AAHH!

NIP-NERF Grab with thumb and forefinger, squeeze hard, then twist like you're buying a gum ball. Pay no attention to screams of pain.

Here's the other thing about Kamikaze: It's kind of skeezily funny the first two or three times. But the next nine hundred? Not so much. Especially if you get caught in the wrong place at the wrong time. Which reminds me, here's another question for you:

What's worse, getting poison ivy or getting poison oak?

If you answered "getting both at the same time," then you're starting to get the idea of what my first week at Camp Wannamorra was really like.

CHAPTER 16

THERE IS A HEAVEN

Truth time. If I'm being honest, I have to say that camp wasn't *all* bad.

I had some new friends, for one thing. I didn't have to see my sister most of the time. And best of all, from 2:05 to 3:05 every day that it didn't rain, the boys' camp got to use the waterfront.

To tell the truth, camp wasn't all bad. It was okay between 2:05 and 3:05. Except on rainy days. Then it was all bad.

The lake was probably the one thing at Camp Wannamorra that actually looked better in person than in the brochure. Honestly, it was kind of awesomely beautiful. If you passed the water safety test, you could swim off the dock and out to the raft. You could use the canoes and rowboats. Or you could just lie around and look at Katie Kim.

Yeah, that's right. I didn't even mention the *best*-best part yet. Guess who was one of the lifeguards?

She took this little motorboat from the girls' side of the lake back and forth every day. If I ever figured out how to make actual words come out of my mouth when she was around, I was going to ask her for a ride. In the meantime, I really liked being in the water and hanging out on the raft, which was my favorite spot in the whole camp.

So of course, Doolin and the Bobcats had to wreck that too.

There I was, all by myself on the raft one day, soaking up the sun and feeling like life could be worse, when I heard Katie laughing over on the dock. When I looked, Doolin was there too. He said something and she laughed again. Oohh—that gave me a migraine *and* a stomachache!

I knew we were just kids to Katie, but still, more than anything I wanted to make her laugh like that. Stupid Doolin was blabbing away like it was the easiest thing in the world. How do guys do that? Talk to girls, I mean. Seriously, is there some instruction manual I never got in the mail?

And because I was so busy sending virtual
sharkgrams Doolin's way, I didn't even notice the
other Bobcats coming up behind me. The next
thing I knew, I felt a cold, wet foot under my back,
and I got rolled off the raft like this was some kind
of burial at sea.

"Our turn," somebody said.

When I got the water out of my eyes, I saw three of them standing there, looking down at me. I didn't even know their names, but I knew they were Doolin's friends.

"Swim on back to shore, Muskrat Meat," one of them said. "You rodents like the water, don't you?"

"You Bobcats like being world-class dinguses, don't you?" I said.

"Come up here and say that."

I actually wanted to. I wanted to climb right back onto that raft and start swinging with my lethal fists. But there were a few problems with that plan.

One, I don't have lethal fists.

Two, I didn't want to risk getting in trouble with Katie or getting permanently kicked off the waterfront for fighting.

And three, it also might have had something to do with the four hundred pounds of Bobcat on the raft, and the one hundred pounds of wet Muskrat in the water. "You and your Muskrats are going to pay for that crack!" one of them yelled at me as I swam away.

And something told me those world-class dinguses weren't kidding.

CHAPTER 17

RETURN TO LOSERVILLE

S ure enough, that night after dinner, we came
back to the Muskrat Hut and found it was a
disaster area—like maybe a hurricane or a tornado
had hit our home away from home.

On the outside, the cabin looked normal. But
when we went inside and turned on the light, it
was like there'd been an explosion at a shaving
cream factory.

It was everywhere—on the floor, on the windows,
on the beds. *Especially* on my bed.

And that wasn't all. They'd gone after Norman,
big-time. Besides the shaving cream, there was tape
all around his bunk, like it was some kind of toxic
waste dump. They'd also put up these stupid signs
that said DANGER and KEEP OUT and BOOGER ZONE.

I looked over at Norman, but he didn't say anything at all. He just started taking down all the tape and signs and throwing them away. I figured the least I could do was help him clean up. Technically, it was my bunk too. Not to mention, this was at least partly my fault.

Still, once I started touching his sleeping bag and stuff, I couldn't help but think about that stupid name, Booger Eater, and what it might really mean.

It must have shown too, because Norman took one look at me and said, "You don't have to worry, Rafe. I stopped eating my boogers when I was six."

"Oh," I said. "I wasn't thinking about that....I mean, I wasn't—"

"Yeah, you were," he said. "It's okay."

I just kept wiping up shaving cream with my towel, but I still wondered what he was thinking. After another minute, I said, "So then...why do you let people call you that?"

"Let them?" he said. "It's not exactly my choice. I got caught doing it once, six years ago, and it just kind of stuck."

"Like a booger," I said. That actually got a smile out of him. "But doesn't it bother you?"

Norman shrugged. "Whatever," he said. "It doesn't matter. I don't even care that much."

This kid was a terrible liar. I could see right through him. He was acting like he didn't care because he didn't think he could do anything about it. But I would have bet anything that he cared a whole lot—on the inside.

Been there. Done that.

"What if I came up with a different nickname?" I said. "I could call you Boo, for short. You know, instead of Booger—"

"I got it," he said. "And no thanks."

"What about Norm?"

"My name's *Norman*, Rafe," he said. He crumpled up the last of those stupid signs and tossed them in the wastebasket. "It's not that complicated."

I tried to look him in the eye. "That's the same thing you said about the math," I told him.

But I guess he was done talking. He just climbed onto his bunk and picked up another book. This one was called *The Lord of the Rings* by some guy named J. R. R. Tolkien. I think the R. R. stood for "Reading and Reading" because this book looked about ten thousand pages long. I couldn't finish

that book in my lifetime, but Norman would probably be done by breakfast. It was crazy.

Almost as crazy as he was. I seriously didn't get
him, but I did feel bad for him. And let's face it, if he
hadn't been at Camp Wannamorra, it would have
been me down there at the bottom of the heap.
Usually, that's what the new kid is *for*.

Maybe I should have just minded my own business. Maybe it would have been better for everyone if I'd left it alone. But I couldn't stop thinking
about how Norman was going to be stuck with that
nickname for the rest of his life if someone didn't
do something about it.

Someone like…oh, I don't know. Me, maybe.

CHAPTER 18

TIME-OUT

Time-out for a second.

In case anybody's wondering, the answer is NO, I did not have a new mission. I'm totally out of the mission business.

For more information on Operation R.A.F.E. and Operation: Get a Life, consult these EXCELLENT books. This is not an ad. It's a public service announcement. You're welcome!

I'd already done two gigantic missions with Leo. The first was Operation R.A.F.E. (Rules Aren't For Everyone), and it got me into a whole lot of trouble. The second one was Operation: Get a Life, and guess what? It got me into a whole lot of trouble too. Even I could see a pattern there.

So was I interested in a new mission? No. Absolutely not. Wasn't going to happen.

No way.

No how.

No, sir.

No sale.

Just...no! No! NO!

MIDDLE SCHOOL MY BROTHER IS A BIG, FAT LIAR

"My mission was to write a book one hundred times BETTER than Rafe's book. Mission accomplished."
—Georgia Khatchadorian

CHAPTER 19

BUT...

But if I *did* have a new mission, it would have been called Operation: Norman. That's all.

Now turn the page and forget I ever said anything.

(And definitely forget my sister Georgia's ridiculous plug for her ridiculous book.)

"Nice try, small fry."
-RK

CHAPTER 20

TAKE A HIKE!

The next day at lunch, the counselors told us that the Muskrats, the Bald Eagles, and the Badgers were all going on a nature hike. It meant missing out on the waterfront, but at least the Bobcats weren't going to be there.

We went back to our cabin, got our stuff, and headed out into the woods.

Now, I like nature as much as the next guy. In fact, I like it a lot.

I like hiking too.

But it turns out that when you put those two together to make "nature hike," it's like putting pickles in a pudding cup. Bad combination of two perfectly good ingredients.

It probably doesn't have to be that way. (The

nature hike, I mean, not the pickles and pudding.
The one time I tried to make Georgia eat that, she
almost threw up.)

(What? You thought I was going to try it myself?)

The thing about nature hikes at Camp Wannamorra is that they're led by the head counselor,
Chuck—also known as Wood Chuck, Up Chuck,
and most of all, Boring Chuck.

He was one of the science teachers in the morning, which meant he knew everything there was to know about every leaf, bush, tree, bird, and bug within a hundred miles of camp. Make that five hundred miles.

And *that* meant instead of getting the afternoon off from school, we were hiking right back into it.

Sometimes my teachers, or even my mom, will ask me why I'm always spacing out and making up stuff. All I can say is that sometimes life is a whole lot more interesting inside my head than it is on the outside.

In fact, why don't you come on in, and I'll show you around, Khatchadorian-style. You want a nature hike that *doesn't* put you to sleep? Follow me.

Now if you come right down here through the woods, you'll get a nice view of Lake Wannamorra, just in time to catch the camp mascot, Heads and Tail. He's the two-headed, slime-eating, slime-spewing beast that surfaces from the bottom of the lake once a day to empty his snot pockets all over the people we don't like. (That's right, Doolin, I'm talking about you.)

Oh, and look up there in that tree. It's Ugg and Lee, the most hideous-looking crows you've ever seen. They're either brothers or sisters, I'm not sure which. It's hard to tell with crows. But their song is sweeter than a slice of apple pie with extra cinnamon. This next tune goes out to Katie Kim.

Okay, everyone, we're coming into a rougher part of the forest now, so watch your back. Right over there, I can see Bucko the Deer, Bambi's cousin from the wrong side of the tracks. He looks innocent enough, but don't let those big eyes fool you. This deer-dude is armed and dangerous, and he'll steal your lunch money just as soon as look at you.

Of course, Bucko's nothing compared to what you *don't* see around here. Meet Snake, Rattle, and Roll, just three of the zillion venomous killers waiting for you in the shadows if you're unlucky enough to stumble onto Snake Hill.

If you ever *do* come face-to-face with one of these guys, it's probably because they already have their three-inch fangs in you, and you've got just enough time left to wish you'd done arts and crafts that day instead of hiking.

So let me give you a tip: When you find yourself lost and alone on Snake Hill, there's one thing you can do to protect yourself. Just one thing that can save your life, so listen very carefully. First, you have to—

"Rafe?" Boring Chuck said. "Are you even listening to me?"

"Yeah," I said.

"What was I just saying?"

"Uh...something about leaves?"

"That was ten minutes ago. I was saying we have to turn around and go back now."

I looked up at the sky and saw a bunch of dark clouds. The wind was kicking up too, and it was just starting to rain.

"Sorry, fellas, it looks like we won't make it all the way to Snake Hill today, after all," Chuck told us.

I was kind of disappointed, actually. I was just starting to get into this whole nature hike thing.

CHAPTER 21

TUNA SURPRISE

When we got back to the Muskrat Hut that day, we had another surprise waiting. Not the good kind of surprise, of course. More like the smelly tuna-and-sardine kind.

"*What is that?*" Bombardier said, before we even got up the steps. He had the best sniffer of anyone, which is funny when you think about it.

But there was nothing funny about the inside of the cabin. It smelled like one giant fish market, with extra fish.

"Oh, man! I've got tuna under my bunk!" Cav yelled out.

"Sardines over here," Smurf said.

When I looked under mine, there were sardines *and* tuna. Lots of it.

The "Cool Cabin" had struck again. Shaving cream, old fish...what was next?

"I don't get it," I said. "What do those guys have against us?"

"Everything," Tunz said.

"We tried talking to Major Sherwood once," Cav said.

"But he thinks it's all 'good clean fun,'" Smurf said. "You know how he's always saying Camp

Wannamorra men work things out for themselves? Well, this is what he's talking about."

It was weird. I felt like they were all saying the same stuff Norman had said about his nickname—how it's always been that way, and there was nothing we could do about it, and blah-blah-blah.

But I wasn't ready to just roll over, play dead, and go home at the end of the summer smelling like tuna, sardines, and defeat. It was time for us losers to start sticking together.

This was it. They weren't going to push us around anymore. It was time to push back. Hold our ground! Get revenge...

…just as soon as we cleaned up all that fish.

"Listen, guys," I said. "We have to do something about this."

"What do you mean, like air freshener?" Bombardier asked.

"No. I mean—well, maybe that too," I said. "But we're not going to let Doolin and the Bobcats walk all over us anymore."

"What are you saying?" Dweebs asked. "You mean they're going to *run* all over us?"

All of a sudden, everyone was looking at me. Even Legend, I think, but I didn't have the nerve to look back, especially since I didn't have a plan yet.

But I did know where to start. First things first. (And I don't mean the fish.)

"Who's up for a little reconnaissance?"

CHAPTER 22

RECONNAISSANCE

We waited until after lights-out that night. Then we waited some more, for Rusty's bunk check at eleven thirty. We'd all gone to bed with our clothes on, so as soon as we heard him whistling his way back down the path, we were good to go.

Everyone went except for Norman. The seven of us left him at the Muskrat Hut and took off. We went around behind the cabin, then up through the woods, so nobody would see us on the trail. It also gave me a chance to talk about Norman.

"You guys should stop calling him Booger Eater," I said, once we were out of earshot. "I don't think he likes it. Who would?"

"I guess," Smurf said. "It's just kind of always—"

"Yeah, yeah. That's how it's always been," I said.

"So what? We know who the enemy is now. I say we focus on them."

"Yeah. One for all, and all for nothing!" Dweebs said.

"Duck, Dweebs!" Tunz said.

"What?"

I heard a clunk in the dark. That's when Dweebs hit his head on a branch. The kid lives at a different altitude than the rest of us, that's for sure.

"I'm just saying, it wouldn't hurt anyone to call him Norman once in a while," I told them.

"*Shh!*" Smurf said.

We were just about to come out of the woods. Our cabin was way back in the trees, but Bobcat Alley was right out in the open. If we wanted a good look at this place, we were going to have to commando-crawl into the middle of the main field and make like pancakes in the grass.

Even then, there was no way to get too close without being seen. That place was like a fortress.

"What are we looking for?" Cav whispered.

"*Shh!*" Smurf said.

"Don't *shh* so loud!" Dweebs said.

"Is anyone going to answer my question?" Cav said. "*What are we looking for?*"

"Anything we can use," I whispered.

The truth was, I didn't know. There was only so much plan I could come up with ahead of time. So we waited. And watched.

And watched. And waited.

After a while, it started to feel less like spying and more like lying in the wet grass watching nothing happen.

But then, all of a sudden, a line of shadows came out of the woods, heading straight for Bobcat Alley.

"Who's that?" Dweebs said.

"Shh!"

There were four of them. At first, I thought it was some kind of sneak attack, but then the shadows walked right up the steps and into the cabin. Once they were inside, another four came out and headed toward the same part of the woods.

I could hear Doolin with them too, and my brain kind of sizzled like a frying pan. I *really* didn't like that kid!

Then I saw someone flick a lighter in the dark. It was just for a second before they disappeared into the woods. That lighter meant they were doing one of three things: lighting stuff on fire, setting off

fireworks, or smoking—and I hadn't seen anything
burning or heard any explosions from the woods.

What a bunch of idiots! Who in
their right mind would smoke?

"Should we follow them?" Smurf asked. "I think
we should follow them."

"Not yet," I said. "We just found their weak
spot. Next time we come back, we'll hit them hard.
They'll be sorry they ever messed with us. Am I
right?"

"Um…"

"I guess."

"I doubt it."

I was just about to tell the guys to man up a little when I heard this horrible, scary growling noise

in the dark....To be totally honest, I almost wet my pants.

"*What was that?*" I said.

"Is it a bear?"

"I don't want to die!"

"*Shh!*"

"Sorry, guys," Tunz said. "That was my stomach. I'm starving."

Phew! I was glad to hear that. In fact, I was starving too.

"Where can we get something to eat around here?" I asked.

"Supposedly, there's a kitchen in the counselors' dorm," Cav said. "I hear they've got some bodacious snacks."

"*They do*," someone said.

At first, I didn't even recognize the voice. Then I realized it was Legend who'd said it.

Everyone stopped and tried to look at him in the dark, but he didn't give any more details. And nobody asked. It seemed safer that way.

Meanwhile, I was still starving.

"So...where is this place with the bodacious snacks?" I asked.

CHAPTER 24

THE DICTATOR

Major Sherwood was not amused. He marched us all double time to his personal cabin to begin the interrogation.

As we came up to the ominous cabin, I got to thinking about what kind of torments Sherwood used to pry confessions from suspects, and then *WHAM!* Suddenly, I'm a head on a wall.

"I told you we didn't want to get on his bad side," Dweebs whispers to me, just before—
FWAP! He gets a riding crop to the cheek.

"No talking!" the Dictator screams. "Understand?"

"Yes, sir," I say, right before—*FWAP!*

"I said NO TALKING! *Understand?*"

I understand, all right. I may be down to just a head, but something tells me this guy hasn't done his worst yet. I'm going to be lucky to make it out of here with two eyes, a nose, and a mouth.

"I have one question," he says. "Whose idea was this?"

Nobody says anything. Nobody even breathes. While he waits for an answer, the Dictator paces back and forth like a restless lion. And then, because that's just how my luck goes, he stops right in front of me.

"It was you, wasn't it?" he asks. "Mr. Whatcha-macallit."

I shake my head no, because (a) I've already learned my lesson about talking in here and (b) there's nothing else left to shake.

"LIAR!" he screams, sending a spray of spit and the last bits of whatever he had for dinner in my face. It smells like beef jerky, but for all I know, it's camper jerky, made from the last kid to cross this guy.

"Do you know what I could do to your family?" he asks. "To *you*?"

I nod, because yes, I have a pretty good idea about that by now.

"We have laws around here for a reason. Do you understand, Whatchamacallit?"

I keep nodding like my life depends on it— because it probably does. The spit's flying so fast, I'm also wishing for those glasses with the little windshield wipers on them.

"I won't have it, Whatchamacallit, do you understand? I won't have it! All of my boys were good, law-abiding subjects before you came along...."

I want to say, *Excuse me, but have you met Legend? Or Doolin? Or any of the other hostile creeps running around this place?* But instead, I just keep snacking on my tongue.

"...so consider this a warning—your first and

your last. Lucky for you, I'm feeling generous tonight. Have you got that?"

Nod, nod, nod…

"You may thank me now."

"Um…thank you?" I say.

"Now all of you—GO! Roll on out of here before I change my mind," the Dictator roars.

He doesn't have to ask us twice. And because that's the only thing we *can* do, we get rolling while the rolling is good.

CHAPTER 25

CONFINED TO QUARTERS

Major Sherwood might've called it "confined to quarters," but I know a suspension when I see one. That whole next afternoon, we had to stay put in our cabin and "think about what we'd done."

The big surprise was that Norman hung with us all day, even though he wasn't in trouble.

"Thanks for sticking around, NORMAN," I said, about six times before anyone got the hint. "That's really cool of you, NORMAN."

"Thanks, Norm," Bombardier told him.

"It's *Norman*," Norman said, without even looking up. I'd have to talk to him later about meeting the guys halfway. Still, it seemed like progress.

Then he jumped down, went over to unlock his trunk, and started going through the wall-to-wall books inside. I swear, he didn't even have room for extra underwear in there. It was just a library in a box.

"Here," he said, and tried to hand me this three-inch-thick book.

"No, thanks," I said. "I'm not *that* bored."

"You like art, right?" he said. "You'll like this. And the story's good too."

The name of the book was *The Invention of Hugo Cabret*. There were still too many words but also a ton of awesome art. By the time I put it down again, I'd gotten all the way to page 131, which I think would have made Ms. Donatello back home—not to mention my mom—think the world had just turned upside down.

In fact, the only reason I stopped reading at all was because I'd promised Mom and Grandma I'd write them a real letter at least once a week. So far, I'd been at camp for almost two weeks. That meant I still had…almost two letters to write. (Oops.)

But Norman said I could hang on to the book for later. I think he was actually trying to thank me for the whole "Norman" thing.

Of course, only *he* would try to do that with a book. But whatever.

CHAPTER 26

Dear **MOM** and Grandma **DOTTY**,

How are you? I hope you're doing okay. You probably already got about twelve letters from Georgia, so I won't bore you with too many details. Everything is good. You don't have to worry about me.

In fact, guess what? I have a whole bunch of new friends. I think you'd like them (except maybe this kid Legend, who nobody really gets). We're practically the most popular cabin at camp. These guys are great.

Who cares? I like them anyway.

COOL-O-METER

coolest

not cool...

MUSKRATS RULE

School is going okay. I'm learning a whole lot. And maybe you should sit down for this part, because you're never going to believe it. Guess what I was just doing before this? Reading a book. It wasn't even one they made me read, and I got through a whole inch and a half of it, just today. So who knows, maybe anything's possible.

Actually, that part's true.

The food here is great too. Don't worry, Mom and Grandma; it's not as good as yours —or even as good as Swifty's—but I'm eating all my vegetables, so don't worry about that either!

← 5,004th carrot eaten!

Should meat be... gray?

Spit-warm bug juice

Succotash: plenty of "Suc," not enough "tash."

And I saved the biggest surprise for last. I've been kind of hanging out with this girl named Katie. She's really mature, and really, really smart, and a great swimmer too. I know you'd like her.

Knows I'm alive. That's progress right?

D+

Anyway, that's about all the news. I hope your summer is going as good as mine so far. You should know you sent me to an AWESOME camp. And most of all— DON'T WORRY ABOUT ME! I'm good.
Love you, miss you,
Rafe

for you + Dotty

CHAPTER 27

STUPID, IMPOSSIBLE, RiDiCULOUS

So you've probably figured out by now that I couldn't get Katie Kim out of my head. Otherwise, why would I be writing to my *mom* about her?

And yes, I know how crazy that sounds. Basically, I had a better chance of being struck by lightning and winning the Megabucks while a unicorn did my homework for me than I had with Katie Kim. Or with Jeanne Galletta, for that matter.

Not to mention, falling in love with a teacher is a little like falling in love with the enemy, right? But if you know me (and I think you probably do by now), then you know that being REALISTIC isn't exactly my best quality.

In other words, why have one stupid, impossible, ridiculous crush when you can have two?

I couldn't help it. Every time I was anywhere near Katie, it was like she hijacked my brain. I'd be sitting there in math class or floating around on the lake, and I'd just start thinking...and thinking...and thinking....

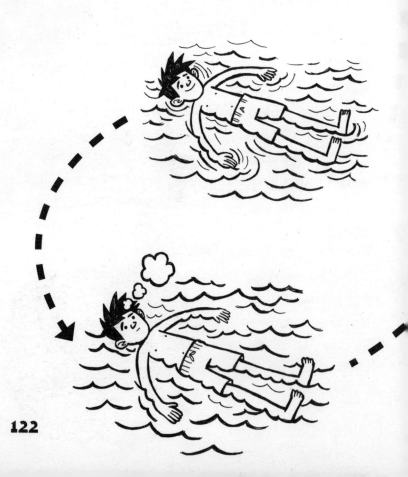

CHAPTER 28

ASSAULT WiTH A DeADLY CANOe

So there I was one day, having a perfectly nice (stupid, impossible, ridiculous) daydream about Katie when I almost got mowed down right in the middle of Lake Wannamorra.

Nope, not the Bobcats. This time it was my own sister.

At first, I wasn't paying any attention. I had my head in the water, and this tiny voice somewhere in the background started going, "Rafe...hey, Rafe...it's me!"

But then without warning, it turned into, "LOOK OUT, RAFE! I DON'T KNOW HOW TO STEER THIS THING!"

When I looked up, all I saw was the pointy end

of a canoe coming right for my face. I dove down deep, swam over to the raft, and climbed up on top to get out of the line of fire. Lucky for me, I'm good in the water.

Georgia was sitting there in the canoe with some girl I didn't know. Both of them had these big life vests on and looked like a couple of giant orange marshmallows—the kind who don't know the first thing about steering a boat.

"What are you doing here?" I asked. "I can't believe they let you out on the lake by yourself."

"I'm not alone—*duh!*" she said. "This is Christine Worley. She's my bunk mate and my new best friend."

As soon as the other girl started talking, I could see why she and Georgia might get along. It was like they had matching big mouths.

"Hi-Rafe-Georgia-already-told-me-all-about-you-are-you-having-a-good-summer-I-am-and-by-the-way-I-think-your-sister-is-totally-the-bomb-I'm-so-glad-we-got-assigned-to-the-same-cabin-because-we're-having-a-really-really-really-REALLY-awesome-time!" she said.

"Hi," I said.

"Christine's brother goes here too," Georgia told me.

"Uh-huh," I said. Katie was over on the dock putting suntan lotion on her nose, and I was watching her, so I wasn't really paying attention.

"His name is Tommy Worley," Georgia said. "Is he in your cabin?"

"Nope," I said.

"Actually, nobody calls him Tommy," Christine said. "Everyone here calls him Doolin...."

And—SLAM! Let me tell you, I didn't see that one coming. It was like getting hit in the head with an invisible fist. This girl was Doolin's *sister*?

I was still taking that one in while she kept talking.

"The Doolin part comes from my mom, 'cause when Tommy was little, he used to play with swords all the time, so she started calling him Dueling Tommy and then Dueling and then it was just Doolin after that. Actually, my brother has a whole bunch of nicknames, like TW and Cheese Steak, and sometimes we even still call him Pamp—"

"Yeah, okay, well, have a good summer," I said.

Then I dove into the water and started making my getaway.

It wasn't like I was afraid of Christine, exactly. I just figured that between her mouth, Georgia's mouth, and my luck, I was better off keeping my distance. One false move, and I'd have the whole Bobcat cabin coming after me even more than they already were.

"Wait!" Georgia yelled after me. "Don't you want to come canoeing with us?"

I turned over in the water and just kept kicking. "No way," I said. "Too dangerous!"

They probably thought I was talking about the canoe. Which was fine with me. The less I said, the better.

Because unlike my sister, I know when to keep my mouth shut.

CHAPTER 29

RAFE TO THE RESCUE
(KIND OF)

When Katie blew her whistle at 3:05, I was the last one out of the water, as usual. I always liked swimming for as long as possible.

That meant I was also usually the last one walking up the path from the lake to the main part of the boys' camp.

And that's where I stepped into my next big, steaming pile of trouble.

The path goes right through the forest, and for about five minutes there's nothing around you but trees. I thought I was all alone that day, but then I heard some voices back in the woods.

When I looked over, I saw Doolin and a couple of his friends giving Norman a hard time. They were tossing this blue towel back and forth, playing keep-away while he tried to grab it.

"Give it back!" Norman said.

"Not until you say it," Doolin told him.

"I'm not going to say it."

"Then you're not getting your towelski back."

I stepped behind the thick branches of a big pine tree to keep out of sight. I wasn't really sure what to do, and I wanted to see what would happen before I made any stupid decisions that maybe could get me and Norman murdered.

"Go on," one of the other guys said. "It's not that complicated. 'Booger Eater would like his towel back. Pretty please.' Just say it."

"Forget it," Norman said. "Keep the stupid towel."

He started to walk away, but Doolin's two friends grabbed him by the arms. I still didn't know those guys' names. I just thought of them as Number One and Number Two (if you know what I mean).

I also saw an empty can and some old cigarette butts on the ground. This was probably where the idiots snuck out to smoke at night like the idiots they were.

"No way, Booger Eater," Doolin told him. "You started this, and I'm going to finish it."

"I didn't start anything!" Norman said.

The one thing he had going for him was that he didn't sound like he was going to cry. That was good. In a weird way, Norman was actually kind of tough. He'd probably been through something like this a million or so times.

And in a *really* weird way, I could relate. I'd been up against my own share of jerks, like my mom's old boyfriend, Bear, and Miller the Killer, and Zeke McDonald. I guess I never would have survived this far in middle school if I weren't at least a little bit tough myself.

But meanwhile, I couldn't just walk away and leave Norman on his own.

The question was, what to do now? As usual, I had plenty of ideas. Just not good ones.

Then, before I could figure out a real plan, I leaned out to see better, and that's when I totally blew it.

I guess my foot landed on a stick or something, because there was this loud *SNAP!* It went off like a gunshot in the woods. The next thing I knew, I had four pairs of eyes looking my way.

Doolin smiled. Then he laughed out loud. He actually seemed happy to see me.

"Look who it is," he said. "The second-biggest loser at Camp Wannamorra. What's your name again? Whatchamacallit? Katch-a-cold?"

My heart was bouncing around like a pinball by now. This was three against two—at best. I wasn't even sure that Norman and I added up to two.

"Just give him his towel back, Doolin," I said. "What do you care? He didn't do anything to you."

"Here's the deal," Doolin said. He pointed at the towel around my neck. "You can trade if you want. Yours for Booger Eater's."

"His name is Norman," I said, but all that got me was another big horse laugh. I didn't care about my own stupid towel anyway. So I walked over and held it out for Doolin.

"Here," I said. "Take the towel. Satisfied?"

"Rafe, don't!" Norman said, but Doolin already had it. He didn't make any move to give back Norman's.

"Wow. You're even stupider than you look, aren't you?" Doolin said.

Now I was starting to get this familiar feeling inside. It's like when you're halfway up that first hill on the roller coaster and you know what's coming, like it or not. Also known as the "point of no return."

My fingers curled into fists. My face felt like someone had just turned on the heat in the woods. If I had to fight, I'd fight.

"I'm not fooling around, Doolin," I said. "Give me the towels. Right…now."

Did I expect him to listen to me? Nah. It was more like one last try before I took a really dumb swing at him and started getting my butt kicked.

The point of no return

But then the unexpected happened. The *very* unexpected. The *miraculously* unexpected.

Doolin looked over at his friends—and kind of shrugged both his shoulders. "You know what? We've got better things to do than kick butt here."

Then Doolin dropped the towels, and they all went tromping off through the woods, probably to go make someone else's life miserable.

Just like that.

I couldn't believe it. On the one hand, I never thought that Doolin would actually back down. And on the other hand, I was thinking—

I AM THE MAN!

THANK YOU, THANK YOU!

I AM THE MAN!

I was about to give Norman the first high five of his life when I realized that we *still* weren't alone.

I turned around, and there was Legend. He was just standing on the path, watching us.

And I thought—*Oh.* That made a lot more sense. I *wasn't* the man. Legend was the man. The minute he'd shown up, it went from three against one and a half...to three against one and a half plus one potential serial killer.

"Um...thanks, Legend," I said.

"For what?" he said. "I didn't do anything. Never lifted a finger. Not my style."

I wasn't sure what to say to that, so I didn't say anything. But as soon as Legend started walking away, I could hear that laugh of his. It's not like a *ha-ha-funny* kind of laugh. It's more like a *ha-ha-I'll-kill-you-just-as-soon-as-look-at-you* kind of laugh.

But whatever. I wasn't complaining.

Norman didn't say anything either. He just picked up his towel and headed back toward the cabins. And he didn't thank Legend, and he didn't thank me. Maybe he wanted to fight his own battles.

But later that day, when I came back from dinner, I found something waiting for me on my bunk. It was one of Norman's precious books, sitting there like some kind of present. So I guess maybe he was grateful after all.

Weird.

But grateful.

CHAPTER 30

THE LEGEND OF LEGEND

here were all kinds of strange things at Camp Wannamorra that I didn't even begin to understand—like math, girls, Snake Hill, mystery meat, and Norman. But the thing I was the most curious about by now was Legend. This kid was way stranger than anyone I'd ever known. Or at least, he might have been if I actually knew him. Which I didn't. Because he was so strange.

You see what I'm talking about? No? Maybe a little? Stay with me here, okay?

That night, when Legend left the cabin to go to the latrine (or to go hunt wild wolves with his teeth, for all I knew), I started asking around.

"Hey, Smurf," I said. "What's Legend's deal, anyway?"

"His deal?" Smurf said. "His *deal*?"

"Yeah. Why is everyone so afraid of him? And where did he get that name, anyway?"

Dweebs leaned down off his bunk. "You've been here more than two weeks. How do you not know this stuff by now?"

I just shrugged. I'm pretty used to *not* knowing stuff. Besides, I wasn't going to admit I'd been kind of scared to ask. You never knew when Legend might be listening in.

"Hey, Cav, check the door," Smurf whispered. "And hit the lights too."

Everyone gathered around on the bottom bunks, except for Norman. His flashlight came on the second the cabin lights went out, and he just kept reading.

Smurf turned on his flashlight too. He held it up under his chin, which was funny and creepy at the same time. I like Smurf a lot. Actually, I like all the guys. Even—up to a point—Legend.

"This," he said, "is the legend...of Legend. Listen at your own risk. I'm not kidding."

I laughed when he said that, but I was the only one who did. So I shut up and listened while Smurf started the story.

"They say he was born on Friday the thirteenth. This particular Friday the thirteenth was right in the middle of the biggest electrical storm in a hundred years *and* a solar eclipse," Smurf said in a creepy whisper. "Right away at the hospital, they knew Legend was different—and not in a good way. The first thing he ever did in his life was give the stink-eye to the doctor who delivered him.

"Nobody knows his real name for sure," Smurf said.

"I heard it was Klaus von Munster," Tunz said. "Hey, I'm just sayin' what I heard."

"It's *Walter*," Bombardier said, "but anyone who's ever called him that is dead, so there's no way to prove it."

"It's very possible he never got a name at all," Smurf told us. "Supposedly, his parents were too scared to choose the wrong one. So he just named himself as soon as he could talk."

"The early years are a little hazy," Smurf went on. "Some people say he went to live with grizzly bears in the Rockies. Some say he went out for chocolate milk when he was five and didn't come back until he was eight.

"What we know for certain is that he spent most of third and fourth grades in the state penitentiary. State records show that Legend was the youngest kid to ever be locked up in that place. But nobody really knows what he got locked up *for*."

"Maybe he robbed a bank," Cav said.

"Maybe he killed someone," Dweebs said.

"Whatever it was, his time in prison only made

him smarter, scarier, and more dangerous," Smurf said. "By the time he got out and started coming here to Camp Wannamorra, Legend knew he had two choices. One—play by the rules. Or two—don't get caught. You can probably guess which way he went."

"And to this day, he's never been caught for anything again," Bombardier said.

"What do you mean?" I asked.

"Every summer there's at least one giant bad thing that happens at camp," Dweebs said. "Something that nobody gets busted for—"

"Even though everybody knows who did it," Cav said. "You know what I'm sayin'?"

"Not really," I said.

"A few years ago, there was this counselor who ate some of Legend's trail mix without asking," Tunz said. "That night, the guy got a whole bottle of Ex-Lax in his dinner. He went into the latrine a few hours later and didn't come out until the end of the summer."

"Then there was the

time *somebody* put a cow in the infirmary—" Smurf continued.

"He made a cow sick?" I said. "What'd the cow do to him?"

"*No!*" Smurf said. "It was the nurse he was mad at. She made him sit out of a kickball game when he had a head cold. So that very night, he walked the cow right in there, closed the door, and left."

"Hang on a second," I said. "You guys don't really believe all this stuff, do you?"

Smurf shined his flashlight right in my eyes! "The point isn't whether it's true or not. The point is—*do you really want to find out?*"

I hadn't thought about it that way.

"No," Smurf said. "You don't. Otherwise, you'll end up like...Petey Schwartz."

"Who?"

Everyone was already quiet, but now they all got even quieter. Smurf started whispering again.

"Petey Schwartz was the only kid who ever told on Legend. We don't know what he tried to bust him for, but it obviously didn't work. Two days later, Petey went on a nature hike and 'accidentally' fell off a cliff—"

"I wouldn't say he *fell*, exactly," Bombardier said.

"Either way," Smurf said. "He landed in the hospital with a broken leg and never came back to camp. Not even to get his stuff."

"And Legend was the one who pushed him?" I asked.

"Yes...no...and maybe," Smurf said.

There were still a bunch of important questions

I wanted to ask, but just then we heard footsteps outside. A second later, Legend came strolling back into the cabin.

"So, ummmm…that's how you tie a double knot," Smurf said.

"Ohhh," Tunz said.

"Got it," Cav said.

"Thanks, Smurf," Dweebs said. "Good to know."

Cav turned on the lights, and we all went back to whatever we were doing before.

Because even though Legend was one of us, and probably our best weapon against the Bobcats, he was also…*Legend*. And you could never be too careful around him.

Just ask Petey Schwartz.

CHAPTER 31

TiMe-OUT:
SCORECARD EDiTiON

Yeah, that's right. *Only seven days to go.* Seven days and counting. You haven't forgotten about that part, have you? Because, believe me, it's coming. Hard and fast. With no way on earth to stop it. That's what some folks call *fate*.

Not that I had any idea I was going to wind up getting kicked out of there. In fact, it felt like things were going kind of, sort of, almost so-so, which was at least better than terrible, how it all started.

So let me give you a quick recap. Here's where everything stood at this point, on the Rafe Khatchadorian Scale of 0 to 10.

NORMAN/BOOGER EATER

Norman: On the one hand, some of the Muskrats were actually calling him Norman by now. On the other hand, most of the camp wasn't. And on the other *other* hand, I still didn't understand what Norman was doing in the same classes as me. It just didn't add up.

SCHOOL

School: I mean, come on— it's *summer school*! If Katie Kim weren't one of my teachers, I'd have to give this one a 0.

Reading: That's right—off the charts.

READING

For me, anyway. Not only had I finished that Hugo Cabret book Norman gave me but I'd started reading the next one, *Holes*. I don't think anyone back home would believe in a million years that I was on my second book of the summer. Even I didn't believe it, and I was there.

Bobcats: Mostly, it was all bad news with them. They'd already gotten us bad a bunch of times, and we still hadn't

BOBCATS

managed even a tiny bit of revenge. The only reason I'm giving myself two points is because things had gone a little quiet on the Doolin-and-fiends front. (But just wait. It doesn't stay that way.)

Girls: If daydreams counted, I'd get an 8. But they don't. (I wish!)

So, like I said, everything was just kind of so-so. I was still hoping it would get better, but if you read the beginning of this chapter, then you already know what was about to happen to my "average score." It was going way down.

Just like me.

You ever heard of *below* 0?

DEAR JEANNE GALLETTA

Since I already had out my paper and pen, I figured I might as well keep going.

Maybe I *could* improve my "average score" in the "Girls" category. If Katie Kim was going to be a guaranteed 0, could Jeanne Galletta change my score?

Jeanne was nicer to me than anyone else when I went to Hills Village Middle School, and I was still thinking about her all the time. She wasn't my tutor anymore, and she wasn't my friend, exactly, but she also wasn't *not* my friend. She'd even written me a couple of e-mails when I moved to the city and told me to "keep in touch," whatever that meant. So I wrote her a letter.

Actually, scratch that. I wrote her about six

letters. But that just turned into about six different ways to sound stupid. Or babyish. Or desperate. Or all of the above. Which is why they ended up in the garbage and not in the mail.

Here—see for yourself.

CHAPTER 33

CAMP DANCES SUCK

The next night (six days left and counting) we had our first all-camp dance. I'd never been to a dance before. In middle school, stuff like that was for kids who knew *how* to dance and who also had someone to dance *with*. If Major Sherwood hadn't forced us to go, I would have hung back and spent the night doing something I liked better. Like maybe pulling my teeth out with a pair of pliers.

But right after dinner, they told us to get ready, and we all hiked around the lake over to the girls' side to "have some camp fun." And to "show camp spirit." And to "let off steam."

wheee!

My idea of a good time on a Saturday night

When we got there—we were already late. The music was playing, and the counselors had put up a bunch of crepe paper and balloons. A lot of the girls were dressed up too. Including Georgia. That didn't surprise me. My sister had packed enough stuff when we'd left home to last her until high school.

"Who's that?" Bombardier asked me. "She's kind of cute."

"Dude, that's my sister," I said. "And believe me—she's *not cute*."

Norman went straight for a chair in the corner with his latest gigantic book and a little book-y flashlight. No surprise there.

Legend went off to do God-only-knew-what. Also no surprise.

Tunz hit the dance floor. Big surprise. Because, let me tell you, the big guy can't dance any more than I can. Still, that didn't stop him from doing the booty bounce all over the floor while a bunch of the girls did this "Gray Squirrel" thing.

The rest of us went right for the refreshment table. There was food I actually recognized, like barbecue chips and punch made with ginger ale, instead of the usual mystery meat and bug juice we got at the Chow Pit.

Pretty soon, everybody was evenly divided up. Half of the guys were huddled together on one side of the room, and half of the girls were on the other side. Everybody else was mixing it up in the middle.

That included Doolin, of course. He was chatting up all the girls and dancing and showing off, and they were all acting like he was the best thing since extra cheese on your burger. To tell you the truth, he *was* a pretty good dancer.

Cav said we should all name which girl we liked best. I thought that was kind of like saying which planet we wanted to fly to, because let's face it—we were Muskrats.

Still, I named Betsy Braces, this girl who was in most of my classes. She was pretty, for sure, but I only picked her so I wouldn't have to say Katie Kim. I didn't need the other guys knowing I was practically in love with my math teacher and swimming counselor.

After that, we all stood around eating kind of stale chips, cracking even staler jokes, and flapping in the wind while we waited for the dance to be over. In other words, the whole thing went just about exactly like I expected it to.

That was, until it didn't.

CAMP DANCES (STILL) SUCK

So what's the absolutely, totally last thing you might expect to happen next?

Martian invasion?

Earthquake?

Tsunami?

Blizzard?

Katie Kim asking me to dance?

I can tell you for sure that we didn't have any alien incidents that night. There weren't any natural disasters either. But...

There I was, drinking my fifth—or tenth—cup of punch and pretty much minding my own business, when, out of nowhere, Katie stopped talking to Major Sherwood and started walking across the room with this odd little smile on her face.

Headed.

Right.

For.

Us.

"Um…guys?" Cav said.

"I see her," Dweebs said.

"What do we do?" Smurf asked.

Bombardier farted.

So I guess I wasn't the only kid at Camp Wannamorra with a teeny-weeny crush on Katie, after all. You could practically hear the sweat dripping off the other guys.

And there she was—standing right in front of us.

"All right, you guys," she said. "You can't spend the whole night holding up the walls. Who's going to dance with me?"

"Uh…" Cav said.

"Umm…" Bombardier said.

"Well…" Smurf said.

You know that expression "opportunity knocks"? It was knocking, all right, but none of us knew how to answer the door.

On the inside, I was thinking, *Yes, yes, yes…I'll*

dance with you, Katie! But on the outside, I was still just trying to get my mouth to work.

I knew there wasn't much time. One of the other guys was going to speak up at any second.

This was huge. I was going to go for it.

So I took a deep breath. I looked Katie in the eye.

And I said, "I'll d—"

Unfortunately, that's as far as I got. Just "I'll d—"

Because then I felt this annoying little tap on my shoulder. Kind of a familiar tap. Who dat?

"Hey, Rafe! Do you want to dance with me?"

It was Georgia, showing up at exactly the wrong moment, of all moments in the history of moments. Of course. That's my sister's specialty.

"Yeah, *suuuure*," I told her. Like that was ever going to happen without a court order.

Except Katie didn't hear me say "Yeah, sure"

like "No way." She heard me say "Yeah, sure" like "YEAH! SURE!"

"Omigosh, that is the sweetest thing," she said. "You guys are brother and sister, right? I wish my brother had been that nice to me when I was your age. Rafe, you're a real class act, you know that?"

I think I said, "*Mrglph*."

This was like the definition of an impossible situation. I either had to show Katie that I was the exact opposite of the good guy she thought I was. Or I had to dance with my sister and look as pathetic as it's possible to look at a camp dance.

What would you have done?

You sure about that?

CHAPTER 35

UNFORGETTABLE

And then out of nowhere, *I lucked out!*

There I was on the dance floor, having the worst three minutes (that felt like three hours) of my life, when some kind of commotion started up by the windows. At first, it was just a couple of kids standing around pointing at something outside.

But pretty soon, it started spreading like a brush fire. You could see kids whispering to other kids and more people crowding around to see what was up.

Some of them were laughing. A few girls screamed or screeched. And then everyone was scrambling for the door to check out whatever it was.

That was all the excuse I needed. As soon as

Katie wasn't watching anymore, I dropped my sister like the hottest potato in the history of hot potatoes and headed out like everyone else.

Do you remember at the beginning of the book when I showed you a picture of a flagpole that didn't exactly have a flag hanging on it? Well, that was just part of the whole thing. I was kind of saving the rest.

When I got outside, *this* is what I saw.

Just for the record, this wasn't anywhere near the first time I'd seen ladies' underwear. At home, I live with a whole house full of ladies, and believe me, Grandma Dotty isn't shy about that kind of thing. There's almost always something white and floppy hanging in our bathroom.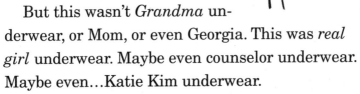

But this wasn't *Grandma* underwear, or Mom, or even Georgia. This was *real girl* underwear. Maybe even counselor underwear. Maybe even…Katie Kim underwear.

And *that's* the part that made my head almost explode.

The whole thing was over pretty quick. One of the counselors started taking down the "flag" while the others herded us all back inside, saying stuff like "Move it along" and "Nothing to see here."

Nothing to see? Yeah, right! That's what they say at car crashes and crime scenes when there's *all kinds* of stuff to see.

Still, we didn't have much choice. By the time we got back inside, they'd already refilled the refreshment bowls and had the music going again, like nothing had happened.

But it didn't take a genius to notice the way Doolin was laughing with his friends or how they were all looking around to see what everyone was doing now.

The Bobcats had struck again, of course. Who else?

I guess I couldn't complain. It got me out of dancing with Georgia. It showed me something I'd never seen before (in a good way). And it meant that Doolin and fiends weren't doing anything to us in the meantime. It seemed like a pretty good deal, actually.

Or so I thought.

In fact, the worst night of the whole summer had already begun.

FOOD POISONING!

The all-of-the-camp, all-of-the-time barfing started around four in the morning.

You know those machines in the hardware store that shake up paint cans? That's about how my insides felt when I woke up. My head was spinning too, and I could tell that all those chips and the punch in my stomach were about ten seconds away from liftoff.

I got out of bed in the dark and bumped right into someone.

"Watch out!" It was Tunz. "I'm gonna—"

"Me too," I said. We both hit the door at the same time and beat it down to the latrines.

It turned out we were wasting our time. I didn't even know the cabin was half empty when I left it.

And the latrines were full when we got there. In fact, they were more than full. There was a line of guys out the door.

Maybe you already know this, but when you're feeling like you're about to blow chunks, it doesn't exactly help to hear someone else doing the deed ahead of you. It just kind of speeds things up.

Or like Tunz so eloquently put it—"barf makes barf."

Now take that idea and multiply it by the whole camp. It wasn't just the kids either. All of the counselors were sick too. Everybody was running around from the latrine to the cabins to the main building to the cabins and back to the latrine, like this totally nutball video game called *Vomit!*

By the time the sun came up, Camp Wannamorra was one giant disaster area.

BEELCCH!
I think I barfed myself inside out.
BLEGH!
I'll never eat pudding again! I'll never eat anything again!
Stop talking about food!!
HURL!
Uh...so how much weight can you carry when you fly?
Welcome To
LAKE BELLYACHE

Back in our cabin, the only people who weren't feeling like empty sacks of skin by now were Norman and Legend. It didn't take long to figure out that they were the only ones who didn't pig out on chips or punch at the dance. Norman had been reading all night, and Legend had been…off doing whatever he wanted, I guess.

"They're saying it was some kind of food poisoning," Norman told us. "It's just as bad over on the girls' side too. It must have been something in the chips or the punch."

"Don't say *chips*," I told him.

"Don't say *punch*," Dweebs said.

"Or anything about food!" Smurf said.

"Don't say *food*!" Cav said.

That's about how the morning went. We mostly hung out in our bunk, just praying we were done running back and forth to the latrine or into the woods or behind the cabin or—you get the idea.

I lost track of time, but somewhere in the middle of the afternoon, and just when I was starting to feel normal again, we got hit with another surprise.

"EVERYONE UP!" Rusty said, coming into the

cabin. "LET'S GO, LET'S GO!"

"What's happening?" I asked. "And please don't tell me we're going on a nature hike."

"Nope." He looked more serious than I'd seen him all summer. "I need you dudes to line up outside. Major Sherwood's coming through the cabin. *Right now.*"

"What for?" Smurf asked.

"Turns out it wasn't just regular food poisoning last night," Rusty said. "Someone put *something* in that punch—"

"Don't say *punch*!" Dweebs said.

"—and Sherwood's determined to find out who it was. Guys, welcome to your first surprise inspection!"

CHAPTER 37

THE DICTATOR'S INSPECTION

The Dictator has ways of making you talk.

Even when you don't have anything to say. Even when you don't know anything.

While a squad of his highly trained officers ransack Muskrat HQ, we're all taken outside. This is scary. And major-league upsetting. And my stomach is still feeling really queasy.

That's when the Dictator starts grabbing us, one by one, for interrogation.

Starting with yours truly.

You're first, Mr. Whatchamacallit. Think before you speak. I made these boots out of the last camper who lied to me.

"All right, Mr. Whatchamacallit," he says. "Think very carefully. Where were you when the poisoning in question occurred?"

"I don't know!" I tell him. How could I possibly know when the food poisoning started?

"LIES!" With the press of a button, he sends a thousand volts of electricity right into me. My whole skeleton vibrates like a body full of chattering teeth.

"I swear-r-r-r!" I tell him. "I don't even know when it happened, so I can't really say where I was, sir…Mr. Dictator…sir."

He gives me another jolt, just for fun, and something tells me he's not done with me yet.

"NEXT!" he roars.

It goes on like that for hours. Days. Weeks. Months. Or maybe about fifteen minutes. It's all just a blur now. Hard to say.

Then, finally, one of the Dictator's guards comes outside.

"Sir! Mr. Dictator! Sir!" he says with a salute.

The Dictator pauses with a terrified fourth grader standing in front of him. "Yes?" he says. "This had better be important."

"I believe we've found something, sir! Evidence."

"Well? What is it?"

"This, sir!" The guard holds up a dark, unmarked bottle of some kind. "We found it wrapped up inside of this," he says. With his other hand, he holds up something white and lacy that definitely doesn't belong to anyone on this side of the lake.

Now the Dictator smiles. "Where did you find those?" he asks.

"In a camper's trunk, sir," the guard says.

"*Which* trunk? *Whose* trunk?" The Dictator sucks back a mouthful of drool. I can tell he's ready for blood. And if I'm not mistaken, he's looking right at me.

This is it! I've been set up! I know it. Good-bye, cruel world! Tell Mom I love her. Tell Jeanne Galletta too. Wait—no. Don't tell Jeanne that. It's just embarrassing. Never mind—

But then, the guard reaches out and points a finger—not in my direction.

Straight at Legend.

CHAPTER 38

SO LONG, LEGEND

Nobody could believe it. Not that Legend had made the whole camp as sick as a dog—but that he'd been *caught*.

As soon as they found that bottle and that bra in his trunk, Major Sherwood took him down to the main building, and they disappeared inside. By the time Legend's parents showed up to get him, the whole camp was hanging around waiting to see what would happen next.

"It's like the end of a...what do you call something that you thought would never end?" Dweebs said.

"An era," Norman said. For once, he was hanging out with us. Even he seemed kind of surprised about this, and Norman didn't usually show a whole lot of emotion.

The other thing that was hard to believe was Legend's parents. I kind of figured they were going to look like this:

Sorry we were late, son. My broomstick was in the shop.

Legend's lunch

Or like this:

Or at least like this:

But they were just like everyone else's parents. They didn't even seem afraid of Legend. In fact, they looked pretty darn mad.

When Legend came outside, he didn't look around or say good-bye or anything at all. He just got in the backseat of his parents' car and waited while his parents finished with Major Sherwood. A minute later, they were pulling away, leaving camp forever. Almost everyone was there to watch him go. It was like a major event.

I didn't even notice Doolin and the other Bob-cats until it was over. They were all hanging out by the sports shed, sticking to themselves. The thing was, they weren't watching Legend leave. They were watching us *stay*. And they had these meat-eating grins on their faces, like they were all thinking the same thing.

I may not always be the fastest car on the track, but as soon as I saw the way those guys were looking at us, I started to figure it all out. This was a huge conspiracy.

Legend hadn't done any of this. *They* had.

The whole flagpole thing was just a distraction. It got everyone looking the other way while Doolin or somebody dumped whatever it was into the punch bowl at the dance. After that, it wouldn't have been too hard to plant some fake evidence in the bottom of Legend's trunk. Or to tip off Major Sherwood about who the "real" criminal was.

And guess what? They'd pulled it off. The conspiracy worked.

Now, with Legend out of the way, the only thing standing between the Bullyboys and our complete destruction was...well, nothing.

Which I think was the whole point: We were now officially Dead Meat Walking.

CHAPTER 39

THE DEAD MEAT THREAT

Have you ever lived under a Dead Meat threat? You're nervous and afraid every minute of the day. Kind of like when bullies say, "Meet you after school. We'll settle this with our fists!"

Only this was more like: "Meet you anywhere, anytime we want, and we'll settle this with our fists—or maybe rocks, ball bats, hockey sticks, weapons of mass destruction."

Actually, the Bobcats didn't wait around very long. First thing the next day, they started in with the...

When I woke up, all of my shoes were gone.

Bombardier got hit with a bucket of water in the latrine.

Cav got hung by his boxers on a doorknob.

And that was all before breakfast.

When I told Rusty about my shoe problem, he thought it was totally hilarious. He said this one was a "classic."

"Believe me, dude, those shoes'll be back. Don't sweat it too much. That's like begging for more," he told me.

Then he let me take a pair of world's oldest sneakers out of the lost and found and sent me off to class. I didn't tell anyone else, because it was kind of embarrassing, and I didn't expect them to do anything about it anyway.

Which they didn't.

In the afternoon, Smurf's sleeping bag got thrown way up in a tree.

Then Dweebs got stripped and pushed out in front of the girls at the waterfront.

And just before dinner, Tunz got hit with two shaving-cream balloons.

I never saw who threw them, but I didn't really have to. I was reading the Bobcats loud and clear. We all were. And they weren't done with us yet.

Dead Meat Walking.

CHAPTER 40

CHARLIE BROWN MAY BE A GOOD MAN, BUT DOOLIN SURE ISN'T

The only person who hadn't gotten seriously punked by now was Norman. Not that I thought the Bobcats had forgotten about him. It was more like they were saving the worst for last.

That night was the camp play, *You're a Good Man, Charlie Brown*. And just like with the camp dance, we all had to go.

Was it any good? Let me put it this way: If you took a car wreck, a stink bomb, and a bunch of seriously awful singing and somehow mixed them all up together in a blender, you *might* have something about as bad as that show.

I'm not saying I could have done any better,

but…well, yeah, maybe I could have. It was that bad.

The big surprise for me was that Georgia was in it. She was Sally, Charlie Brown's sister, and had her own song and everything. I didn't even know that until I saw her up onstage. I guess, being at camp, there were even more chances to ignore my sister than usual.

And even though Georgia was just as terrible as everyone else, she was *not* the worst thing about the play.

That would be Doolin. He played Snoopy, wearing this stupid hoodie and dark glasses like he was too cool for it all. And he hardly ever left the stage.

I had to sit and watch him the whole time while all the girls clapped and cheered and acted like he was creating world peace and global cooling up there.

Then, just when it seemed like the play was finally going to be over soon, Doolin had this song called "Suppertime." Charlie Brown brings a dog dish out on stage, and Snoopy sings about how much he can't wait to eat. Yeah, yeah, whatever, whatever.

First, Doolin started singing in this weird voice,

like he had a cold or something. Then he took off his shades and put on big, thick glasses instead. Someone tossed him a huge book from offstage.

That's when I started to get it. He was making fun of Norman—or at least, some version of him. The Booger Eater version.

Sure enough, at the end of the song, Doolin turned around with his back to the audience and took off his hoodie, so we could see the T-shirt he was wearing.

Then he pretended to dig way up inside his nose, pull something out, and start chowing down on it, big-time. All while 90 percent of the audience was screaming and laughing like it was the funniest thing they would ever see in their lifetimes.

Not me. I thought it was the crummiest, meanest thing I'd ever seen.

When I looked over at Norman, he was just staring straight ahead, not doing anything at all. And I started thinking—wouldn't this be a great time for someone like him to pull out his inner Hulk, if he had one?

Because you know what happens when that Hulk guy gets mad, right?

And maybe with Norman, you don't even notice it right away. But if you look closely, you can see his eyes are just starting to turn yellow.

His skin starts to go green, and a low growl comes up from somewhere deep inside him.

"Norman…angry," he says. "Very…angry."

"Huh?" I ask, because he's just mumbling. But he's also too busy to answer. He's getting bigger by the second. His muscles are up to four times their usual size.

(Oh, right. This is Norman we're talking about. So let's say *twenty* times their usual size.)

Of course, nobody's paying attention to Doolin anymore. They're all sitting there with their mouths hanging open.

And before any of them can say, "Who knew?" Norman's out of his seat. He jumps seven rows of chairs in one bound and lands smack in the middle of the stage.

Even Doolin gets it by now. He tries to hide in Snoopy's doghouse, but guess what, Doolin? It's just a prop. That door is painted on, and you've got nowhere to go.

"Snoopy...STAY!" Norman says.

Half a second later, Doolin's wearing a giant green fist for a dog collar.

"Snoopy...BAD DOG!" Norman says, and shakes him like a gallon of fresh-squeezed orange juice.

And because everyone else at camp has secretly hated Doolin all this time, they're starting to clap and laugh and cheer for more.

"Snoopy...FETCH!" Norman says. Then he takes aim and drop-kicks Doolin right through the hole in the roof. (Well, I mean, *now* there's a hole in the roof. There wasn't a second ago.)

And the audience goes bonkers. There's more clapping...

...more cheering...

...more laughing...

...and—

SKREEECH! SLAM!

Meanwhile, back on Earth...

—we're back. Unfortunately, all of that was inside my head. All the best stuff usually is.

Except for the cheering, I mean. That was real, because Doolin had just finished his song, and almost everyone was going crazy over it while Norman just sat there.

Finally, Major Sherwood stood up in the front row. "All right, all right," he said. "Enough of the razzing. Let's get on with the show."

And I thought—*Razzing*? That's what Sherwood thought it was? That's like watching someone get attacked by a shark and then saying, "All right, all right, enough with the nibbling."

Then, as soon as the play started going again, Norman got up and walked right out of the theater.

Poor kid.

I followed him.

CHAPTER 41

THE WHOLE TRUTH
AND NOTHING BUT

Here's something I think about sometimes. I wonder if bullies like Doolin and his fiends ever feel really bad about what they do? And if they don't, why the heck not? What is wrong with these idiots?

Anyway, I finally caught up with Norman back at the cabin. Rusty watched me go. I think he was okay with it. Maybe he even understood how Norman must have felt?

"Go away," Norman said when I came in. He was already on his bunk with a book but not really reading. He didn't even have his glasses on.

"Doolin's a world-class butt-wipe. We both know that," I said. "Don't worry about him."

"I'm not worried," he told me, but it sounded like he was trying not to cry.

Maybe I should have let it drop right there. But I didn't.

"Can I ask you a question?" I said. "Why do you even come to this camp? It sure doesn't seem like you're having any fun. And don't say it's because you need extra school, because I'm pretty sure you've got the biggest brain in the whole camp."

Norman rolled over then and looked me right in the eye.

"Do you seriously want to know?" he asked.

"I swear I won't tell anyone," I said. That's not what he asked, but I think that's what he meant.

Finally, he sat up and put down the book.

"I guess you could say my dad's not a very nice guy," he said.

"Oh," I said. And then, "Wait. What do you mean?"

"Well…he doesn't have a job, for one thing," Norman said. "If I was home all summer, it would just be him and me, every day, and we don't really get along. He says he yells at me to toughen me up, but I think it's just 'cause he's mad all the time."

"Mad at *you*?" I said.

Norman shrugged. "I think he wanted a different kind of son," he said.

I kind of knew how he felt. It made me think of Bear, my mom's old boyfriend who used to live with us. He never had a job either. He just hung out on the couch, taking up space and telling me what a loser I was.

And I thought—*where do these guys come from, anyway*? Like, if we had summer school for dummies, did they have grown-up school for annoying jerks?

As long as he was spilling, Norman told me all those books of his were from his school library back home. The librarian was kind of a friend (no surprise), and she let him borrow a whole bunch for the summer, as long as he brought them back in the fall. That's why he kept them locked up like that.

It was getting way too heavy inside the cabin. I mean, *seriously* heavy.

"Come on," I said. "Let's do something crazy. You want to run down and jump in the lake?"

"No, thanks," Norman said. He got up and started heading for the door. "I'm going to go back down to the play."

Now I'd heard it all. "Seriously?" I said.

"I can't afford to get in trouble with Sherwood," he said. "Not if it means getting sent home, like Legend."

I couldn't argue with that. Not after everything Norman had just told me. If his dad made him *want* to be at Camp Wannamorra, then it had to be pretty bad.

"Yeah, all right," I said, and followed him outside. "Let's go see how that stupid play ends. Who knows, maybe Snoopy gets run over by a tractor trailer or something."

"He doesn't," Norman told me. "I already read the script."

"Of course you did," I said.

CHAPTER 42

AIR LEO

When a private Air Leo jet pulls up outside the cabin that night, I pretty much know that I'm dreaming. But whatever. It's a good dream. Leo and I haven't talked in a while. So I go with it.

"Hop in," he says. "Let's ride."

I leave the cabin, get into the jump seat, and we take off.

Leo goes out low, straight over Bobcat Alley with an extra burst of fumes, which I appreciate. Six point eight seconds later, we're leaving Camp Wannamorra behind at the speed of sound. It feels good to get away.

"Sorry we haven't talked in a while," I say. Last time I saw Leo, he wasn't exactly happy about the whole summer camp thing.

"Don't worry about it," he says. Then he takes us into a vertical climb, going for maximum altitude. (This is the thing with Leo. It's not like he never gets mad. He just never *stays* mad. And that's why he'll probably always be my best friend.)

When we get up to a hundred thousand feet, I pop my seat belt so I can enjoy the zero gravity for a while. I float over to the plane's galley, where Leo already had a double-cheese, double-pepperoni, double-everything-else pizza in the oven for me. I'm starving, so I hit up the soft-serve machine while I wait. (And by the way, if you've never tried soft serve in zero gravity, I highly recommend it.)

"So catch me up," Leo says over the headset. "How's it going down there? What's the plan for Doolin?"

"Isn't that your department?" I say. "I was kind of hoping you'd tell me."

"I might have an idea or two," he says. Leo *always* has an idea or two. "Give me a minute, and I'll show you."

He practices a few more barrel rolls while I eat chocolate-vanilla swirls out of the air. I'm telling you, life could be worse up here.

Then Leo takes us around and comes in low over Camp Wannamorra again. When I feel the gravity taking hold, I head back to my seat, strap in, and check out the view.

The whole camp is spread out underneath us. There's the Muskrat Hut. There's the lake. There's the main field, right in the middle of it all.

And that's when I start to realize why Leo brought me up here in the first place.

"You see where I'm going with this?" Leo says.

"Sure do," I say. Already, I'm sketching it all out in my head.

"What do you think?" he asks. "Can you take it from here?"

"No problem," I tell him, and that's it. Before I can even box up that extra-extra-large pizza, Leo's reaching over to punch the big red button in the middle of the console. It's the one that says DO NOT PUSH.

The glass dome over my head retracts. The thrusters under my seat start to kick in. Leo levels off the jet, and the next thing I know, I'm popping out of there like one big piece of toast.

I free-fall for about a thousand feet until my chute triggers automatically. Then I grab on to the controls and start navigating back down to the Muskrat Hut.

Tomorrow, I'll tell the guys about the new plan. Meanwhile, I'm going to sleep well tonight. Because now I know what to do.

Thanks, Leo. See you at the end of the summer.

CHAPTER 43

ALL IN

What's this? Is there treasure buried here? Not bodies, I hope?" Cav said when I showed the guys my plan the next day. I'd sketched most of it under the covers the night before and then put on the finishing touches during math class when Katie wasn't watching.

"This is our big move against the Bobcats," I said.

"Yeah, right," Tunz said. "You feeling suicidal or something?"

"I'm serious," I told them. "It's not complicated. All I need is one volunteer. *One volunteer?*"

Actually, I'd already decided it had to be Smurf, since he was the fastest, after me. But if this thing went wrong, then we were all going to pay the price. So I needed everyone to get on board.

LAKE

WATERFRONT

Bobcat
Smoking
Spot

Bobcat
Alley

MAIN
FIELD

Counselors'
Dorm

Major
Sherwood's
Cabin

We See All!

SCHOOL
TENTS

Chow Pit

Right now, they were all staring back at me like I'd asked them to sign up for alligator wrestling or ballroom-dance classes or something seriously awful like that.

"I don't know, Rafe," Bombardier said. "Seems like a bad idea."

"No," I said. "Rolling over and playing dead is a bad idea. We have to make sure those guys get off our backs, once and for all."

"I'm not waiting for it to get better," Dweebs said. "I just don't want to do anything to make it worse."

That's when Norman spoke up. I didn't even know he was listening.

"Oh, you don't have to *do* anything to make it worse," he said. "That's going to happen all on its own."

It was like Norman didn't even know how smart he was. If anybody understood how bad it could get around camp, it was him.

"He's right, you guys. The Bobcats are going to keep coming after us as long as we let them," I said. They all looked like they were starting to get it, but nobody moved or said a word. So I put my hand out in the middle of the group. "Come on. Who's in?"

For a second, I thought they were going to leave me flapping in the wind. Then Smurf reached over and put his hand on top of mine.

"Yeah, okay," he said. "You only die once, right?"

"All right, me too," Tunz said, even though it sounded more like, *Well, it was nice knowing you guys*.

It was the same with Cav, Dweebs, and Bombardier, but pretty soon they were all in.

That just left Norman.

"Hey, Norman," I said, "we're waiting here."

As far as I was concerned, he was going to be part of this group whether he liked it or not. I gave him a heavy stare down until he didn't have any choice but to come over and put his hand in with the rest of ours.

Usually, the guy who puts his hand in first and says things like "Who's in?" is some kind of group leader. I'd never been the leader of anything before.

"We'll do this tonight," I said. "And then maybe we won't have to worry about Doolin or any of his creeps for the rest of the summer."

"I like that part," Smurf said.

"Me too," Cav said.

I think I heard Norman gulp. And Bombardier definitely farted.

"Let's go, Muskrats," I said. "One for all—"

"AND ALL FOR NOTHING!"

(Yeah, yeah, I know....We need a new catch-phrase. I'm working on it.)

LiGHTS, CAMERA, ACTiON!

After lights-out that night, we all got in our sleeping bags with our clothes on. Smurf and I were the only ones who were actually going anywhere, but the other guys wanted to be ready for anything.

It was easier sneaking out this time, with just two of us. But we ran it the same way.

First, we waited for Rusty's eleven-thirty bunk check. Then I counted to fifty—twice—to make sure he was good and gone.

After that, we got out of there as fast as a couple of campers who had just seen a rattlesnake. I even had my stupid lost-and-found sneakers on when I got up, so we could leave right away.

Dweebs let us take his camera, which was nice of him, since there was a chance it wouldn't be coming back in one piece. We also brought flash-lights, just in case, but we weren't planning on using them. And I'd borrowed one of Katie's life-guard whistles from the waterfront.

It wasn't exactly perfect, but it would have to do.

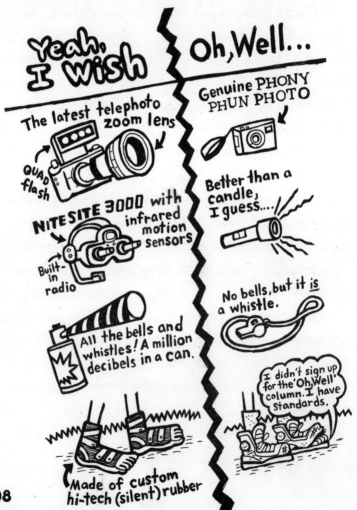

As soon as Smurf and I were outside, we cut straight through the woods and down into the lower part of the main field. Then we stayed low and watched Bobcat Alley for any signs of life, all just like the last time.

It didn't take long. Pretty soon, the door squeaked open and a bunch of them came outside. One guy stayed behind on the porch as a lookout while the rest of them headed off into the woods. Doolin was too smart to leave the cabin totally unguarded.

But he wasn't smart enough to know he was being followed.

Smurf and I kept our distance. We cut around the edge of the field and then tailed the Bobcats down the trail toward the waterfront. About half-way there, they got off the path and headed back into the woods, going for their usual smoking spot.

I could hear them crunching over the leaves and stuff, and I knew from experience that it was too risky to follow them any farther.

But that's what the zoom on Dweebs's camera was for.

Pretty soon, Doolin and the other guys were

lighting up and puffing away like the bunch of moronic losers that they were. I didn't see any reason to wait. I looked over at Smurf. He flashed me a thumbs-up. "Dead meat. You and me, Rafe. Let's go for it!"

Then I stuck that whistle in my mouth, pointed the camera in the Bobcats' direction, and started snapping away like I was with the paparazzi.

"Hey!" one of the Bobcats yelled. "Who's out there?"

"What the—?" another said. I think it was Doolin, but I wasn't really listening. I'd already handed the camera to Smurf, and the two of us took off in opposite directions while I started blowing that whistle for everything it was worth.

Now I just had to get out of this alive.

CHAPTER 45

CATCH AND RELEASE

I guess you could say I was the bait.

Right then, it was more important for that camera to make it out of the woods than it was for me. That's why I headed to the waterfront, making as much noise as I could—while Smurf hightailed it back toward the cabins.

And I guess it was working. I could hear the Bobcats crashing around in the woods, running down the trail behind me. Hopefully that meant Smurf was in the clear.

My first choice was to go around the long way and get back to the Muskrat Hut without getting nabbed. But I was ready for the other possibility too. That was the beauty of this plan. Even my backup had backup.

When I hit the waterfront, I threw the whistle on the dock (thanks, Katie!), then cut left along the water and back into the woods.

At least now I was headed in the right direction.

But running full speed in the woods at night was harder than I thought. And it hurt too. On top of that, I could hear the Bobcats getting closer, coming at me from every direction. They'd split up, which was extra-bad news.

I was just starting to wish for some kind of night-vision goggles when I got blindsided. All of a sudden, there was a light in my eyes, and I couldn't see anything.

I had someone right in front of me and then someone behind me too. Whoever it was grabbed my arm and twisted it hard, until I hit the ground.

"What's the matter with you, Katch-a-cold? You have a death wish or something?"

I recognized Doolin's voice right away.

"Not so much," I said. I started to stand up, but he pushed me back down.

"I think you do," he said. "Seriously—what are you trying to accomplish out here?"

I'm not going to say I wasn't scared. I totally

was. But I still had the upper hand, if I played this right. So I stood up a second time.

"It's already accomplished," I told him. "And if I were you, I'd think twice before you touch me again."

A bunch of the guys laughed at that one, and Doolin got right in my face. He smelled like an ashtray on a bad day, and I kind of wished he'd take a step back just for that.

"So you *do* have a death wish," Doolin said.

"Wrong," I said. "It's called a camera, Doolin. What do you think those flashes were—northern lights? While you guys were out here tarring your lungs, we got all the pictures we needed."

"He's lying," one of the other guys said.

Lucky for me, I wasn't.

"You want to find out?" I said. "Or do you want to stay at camp the rest of the summer? Because I'm pretty sure those pictures would send all of your butts home."

Nobody was laughing now. You could have heard a mouse fart in the woods, it was so quiet. And for once in his life, Doolin didn't have anything to say.

The next thing I heard was Major Sherwood and a bunch of counselors. I could see their flashlights through the trees, and I heard Rusty's voice coming from somewhere near the waterfront.

"So what do you think, Doolin?" I said. "We can settle this with Major Sherwood right now. Or you guys can back off once and for all, and nobody ever has to know about those pictures."

I kind of expected him to deck me right there, but he didn't. So I kept going.

"Oh, and I'm going to want my shoes back too," I said. "Let's say first thing in the morning. *Early.*"

"You are so dead," Doolin said, his mouth frozen in a nasty sneer. "I don't know how yet, but believe me, you're going to pay for this, Katch-a-disease."

"Have a nice night," I told them. Then I just turned around and walked away through the woods. Actually, I kind of floated on air.

I'm not going to lie to you. It was one of the top three best moments of my entire life.

CHAPTER 46

BACK(FIRE) AT THE MUSKRAT HUT

You might say I was feeling pretty good by the time I snuck back into the Muskrat Hut. The only sound I made might have been from my big, swollen head trying to fit through the door.

All the guys were wide awake in their sleeping bags and waiting for me. The lights were off, since another bed check was probably on the way. So I went right for my bunk. Stayed in my clothes. Pulled the blanket up to my chin.

"Well, gentlemen, that was awesome. Smurf, you still have the camera?" I asked.

"Yeah," he said.

"Can I see it?"

"Rafe, we've got a little bit of a problem here," he said.

Believe me, that's not what you want to hear after a night like that.

"What kind of problem?" I asked.

"Look for yourself."

Smurf passed the camera to Cav, who passed it to Tunz, who passed it to me in my bunk. As soon as I turned it on, I almost fainted. Turns out that even after two different art schools, I was still the world's worst photographer.

This didn't even put us back to square one. It was more like square negative forty-two. Doolin and his guys were going to be on the warpath more than ever now.

"What are we going to do?" Tunz said. His big body was shaking like a mountain of Jell-O.

"Pray?" Cav said. "Oh, dear Lord, I beg of you— *mercy.*"

"I say we hit the road," Dweebs said. "Permanently."

"No," Norman said. "Don't do anything."

That shut everybody up. We all knew by now that if Norman bothered talking at all, it was probably worth listening to.

"What do you mean?" I asked. "Do nothing— how?"

"It's obvious," he said. "As long as Doolin thinks we have the pictures, then it's the same as if we did."

And I thought—*that's crazy.*

But then, just as quickly, I thought—*no, that's genius.* It was like Leo smart.

"He's right—again," I said. "If they're already afraid, then we should just let them be afraid."

"But what if—" Dweebs started to say.

"What if *what*?" I said. "Anyone want to walk over there and tell them we *don't* have the pictures?"

The more I thought about it, the more I realized we didn't even have a choice. We had to keep our mouths shut and fake it.

CHAPTER 47

OLYMPiANS!

When I went outside the next morning, my sneakers were sitting on the cabin steps. That seemed like a pretty good sign.

At breakfast, Doolin and fiends watched us like there was poison shooting out of their eyes—but they didn't actually say or do anything.

Same thing in school that morning. I didn't see Doolin (he was one of the Challenge Program brains), but the other Bobcats in my classes kept their distance.

I couldn't say for sure that we had them where we wanted them. It was possible they were working on something. I mean, call me paranoid, but we'd basically left them with two choices: They could back off, or they could kill us in our sleep.

So I wasn't celebrating.

Not until what came next.

After lunch that day, we had the opening ceremony for the camp Olympics. It was supposed to be some huge three-day competition among all the cabins, with prizes for the most medals: gold, silver, bronze, whatever.

I hadn't thought much about it, since I'm not usually the medal-winning type. But the opening ceremony was a big deal. Marching-band music played over the loudspeaker, and all the campers had to line up around the main field with their counselors.

Then Major Sherwood ran out and lit the Olympic torch, which was really just a lantern on a table, but I could tell he took it pretty seriously.

Let the games begin! Everyone's a winner — except the losers. You know who you are, Muskrats.

GAMES

The first event was a gigantic game of dodgeball, which if you ask me is one step away from torture. I'm pretty sure dodgeball was invented by some gym teacher who hated kids and just wanted an excuse to throw things at them.

Anyway, there were a whole bunch of balls in the middle of the field, and as soon as Sherwood said "Go," we were supposed to run in and try to grab one—then start throwing, or dodging, depending on how that went.

If you got tagged (or beaned, or smacked, or knocked unconscious) with a ball, you were out. The last three cabins with guys in the game would win the bronze, silver, and gold medals.

"It's like the beginning of *The Hunger Games*," Norman said. I never saw that movie or read those books, so I didn't know. All I knew was that everyone was already tearing toward the middle of the field to grab a ball, so I took off running myself. If I had to be in this game, it was better to be armed and dangerous than empty-handed and dead.

I would have made it, too, if Norman hadn't distracted me. When I got to the middle of the field, one of the Otters was just taking the last ball, and I had to get out of there, ASAP.

That's when I came face-to-face
with Doolin. Again. And
of course, he was
armed and
dangerous—
and rabid.

For a sec-
ond, nothing
happened. I
looked at him.
He looked at me,
ready to kill.

And then he
hauled off and threw that ball right past me, picking off one of the Not-Bald Eagles with a perfect
shot.

Neither of us said a word. Nada. I just turned
around and kept running. The Muskrats were
dropping like flies, and I didn't think for a second
that we were going to get a medal in dodgeball.

But it didn't even matter. Because I now officially knew that we were safe from the Bobcats—
at least for the time being.

And that was better than gold.

Way, way, way, way, way, way, way, way better.

CHAPTER 48

THE FOULEST EATING CONTEST IN CAMP HISTORY

Next came the biggest, most disgusting event of the day—the annual Camp Wannamorra Eating Contest. Every cabin got to enter two lucky campers, and whoever was left standing at the end got the gold. And probably a stomach-pumping.

We put in Bombardier and Dweebs—who was also the camp's reigning champ. For such a skinny guy, he sure could eat. He probably packs it all in his crazy-long legs.

The Grossathon started with all twenty-four players lined up behind tables in the Chow Pit. Then the counselors brought out twenty-four blueberry pies. The first sixteen campers to get to the bottom of their plates advanced to the next round.

By the way, one of the rules of contest is that you're not allowed to use your hands. If you even touch the food with a pinkie, you're out of the competition.

Sherwood was the official judge. He stood in the middle of the Chow Pit and got the grossness started.

"Competitors ready? On your mark…get set…EAT TILL YOU DROP!"

The campers went at those pies like starving prisoners of war. I couldn't even see anyone's face.

For the first forty-five seconds, it was neck and neck. But then Dweebs started doing his thing.

Breathing? That was for wimps. By the time Dweebs finally sat up—at one minute and thirty-eight seconds—he was practically lapping the field as he had lapped up that blueberry pie.

Bombardier survived the first round too. And they both advanced. Now it was down to sixteen gluttons for punishment.

"Next round!" Sherwood yelled, and the counselors came out of the kitchen carrying bowls of…something very strange and gooey.

"What is that?" I asked Cav.

"Oatmeal and grits," he said. "Every round gets a little harder."

But Dweebs didn't have any problem with the oatmeal and grits either. He came in second this time.

"Don't worry," Smurf said. "He's just pacing himself."

Bombardier lost it in the third round—which was hard-boiled eggs slathered with mayo. He got a beat down from some fifth grader from the Sly Fox cabin. (As far as I was concerned, the less Bombardier ate, the better for everybody in our cabin, considering his specialty.)

We were down to eight campers now. That included one of the two Bobcat dinguses who'd pushed me off the raft that day. The suspense was something else.

"You got this, Dweebs!" I yelled, really getting into it now. I didn't just want him to win. I wanted the Bobcats to lose, and lose big.

I watched every single bite, painful as it was to look at. And you know what? Dweebs did it! I guess the Bobcat kid just didn't have a stomach for chocolate-covered ants.

Now we were down to the final round, with four campers left. They all looked stuffed to the gills—

and even a little scared—as the smirking counsel-ors carried out foil-covered dishes and put them down on the tables.

Even poor Dweebs looked like he was ready to throw up the towel—I mean, throw *in* the towel.

"Here we go," Major Sherwood said. "Don't lift off the covers of your dishes until I say so. Ready? Set? EAT!"

When Dweebs lifted that cover, all I saw was a bowl of green lumps covered in white and sprin-kled with something that looked like it had come off the bottom of a hamster cage.

I found out later that this awful concoction was broccoli, cream sauce, and more ants, but without the chocolate. I'm not kidding—you could hear the whole camp gag at exactly the same time.

Anyway, I won't keep you in too much more suspense, because the final chapter of the Gros-sathon wasn't really that close. As soon as Major Sherwood said "Go," Dweebs went at that glop like it was green M&M's covered in frosting and sprin-kles. I guess you could call that taking one for the team.

Muskrats shoot…score…and win! Dweebs

brings home the gold!

And as for the Bobcats—well, better luck next time.

See you on Day Two, Bullyboys!

CHAPTER 49

LET THE GOOD TIMES ROLL!

We had a really good time in the cabin that night. Winning actually is kind of fun. I had no idea. Rusty brought around brownies and chocolate milk before lights-out. Everybody but Dweebs had some. Even Norman was getting into it.

"Cheers, dudes!" Rusty said, and we all cheered him back on his way out the door.

He probably thought we were feeling good about the gold medal, which was true. But that wasn't all of it.

Y'see, none of us had gotten wedgied all day. None of our beds had been short-sheeted. None of our toilet seats had been covered in butter. Today had been a win-win-win for us.

"Great job, Dweebs," Bombardier said. "And good job, Norman. Way to come up with the big idea."

"Um…thanks," Norman said, like he was embarrassed with everyone gawking at him. But I think he liked the attention.

"What do you think they'd do if they found out?" Dweebs asked.

"Who? The rat-faced Bobcats?" Cav said.

"Yeah. Of course, the rat-faced Bobcats."

"I don't want to think about it," Bombardier said.

"If we don't let them know, then they never have to find out," I said. "As far as they're concerned, that camera's in a safe place and we've already made a jillion backup copies of all those pictures."

"Yeah, the ones that don't exist!" Smurf said, and we all cracked up.

It really was a kind of awesome plan, considering how badly it could have gone.

But here's the thing: My luck stinks. It seems like all I have to do is think, *I've got this*, and then—*BLAM!*

Something blows up in my face.

Or falls apart.

Or goes down the drain.

Or...*crawls under the cabin to spy on us and overhears every word we're saying.*

"What's that noise?" Cav said all of a sudden.

"What noise?" Dweebs said.

"Shh!"

We all stopped and listened. Cav lay down and put his eye up against one of the cracks in the floor.

"What do you see down there?" Bombardier asked.

"Nothing. It's too dark," Cav said.

"Think it's a raccoon?" Smurf said.

"Maybe," Norman said. "I don't think there's enough room down there for a bear."

"A *bear*?" I said.

Just then, something scratched on the floor from the other side. Right under our feet.

Whatever was there, it was moving fast, making some kind of sneaky getaway. My heart was kick-boxing at the inside of my chest, but we all piled outside anyway. I totally expected to see some kind of green-eyed rabid killer grizzly or something.

But it wasn't that at all. It was just a person.

By the time we spotted him, he was already running away, straight up the path. I couldn't see who it was in the dark, but I knew. In my heart, I knew.

"That was a Bobcat!" Smurf said. "A rotten, stinking, spying Bobcat."

"How much do you think he heard?" Tunz asked.

"Who knows?" Smurf said. "Enough!"

"We might still be okay," Cav said. "Maybe he couldn't hear anything through the floor."

"Are you kidding? Are you serious? Are you nuts?" Tunz said. "You can *see* through our floor. What in the name of LeBron James makes you think he didn't hear anything?"

"I guess we'll find out soon enough," I said. But I definitely knew what had just happened—we all did.

The Bobcats had just busted us.
And dead meat was back on the menu.

DEAD MEAT CAFÉ
menu

FILET OF DWEEBS
Charred to a crisp.

SMURF STEAK
Served extra bloody.

BOMBARDIER BURGER
Ground up extrafine.

TUNZ ON TOAST
Served up dead and fresh.

RACK OF RAFE
Served with his own teeth.

CAV NUGGETS
Head, fingers, knees, and toes.

TODAY'S SPECIAL

SLOPPY NORMANS
Beat to a pulp and served on a bun.

CHAPTER 50

RAFE'S PRAYER

I don't know if any of us got much shut-eye that night. We made an emergency survival plan to stay up in shifts and keep an eagle eye out for any sneak attacks, because we were sure one was on the way.

I stayed up with Tunz from ten until one in the morning, but nothing happened. Then we woke up Smurf and Dweebs so we could get some sleep—but that didn't happen either.

Mostly, I just lay there in my bunk, trying to imagine how bad this might get. And as you know, I have some imagination. Plus, let's face it, the Bobcats were some of the meanest bullies ever.

Finally, I couldn't stand it anymore, so I got up to take a walk. I told the guys I was going to the

latrine, and if I didn't come back in fifteen minutes, they should assume the worst: *dead meat down—bleeding from every pore and orifice.*

But I wasn't actually headed to the latrine. I figured it was time to have a serious talk with the Big Guy. And I don't mean Major Sherwood.

The camp chapel was just a tent on the side of the main building. That's where we had services on

Sundays, and even though I'm not exactly an expert, I did like sitting in there on Sundays, thinking about how I'm part of the Big Something Else.

That's what Grandma Dotty calls it. She says it includes anything you can think of—the sky, the stars, the woods, the lake. But also people, like my family and Jeanne Galletta and Ms. Donatello back in Hills Village and all of the Muskrats. Even the Bobcats, I guess. Grandma says if you can look at everything like one gigantic whole thing, then your problems might not seem so big anymore.

Like Doolin, for instance. He may have been the world's biggest dip-wad, but it's not like you could see him from space.

I think that's what Grandma's talking about when she calls it the Big Something Else. Like that's how the Big Guy upstairs sees everything. (I mean...maybe. What do I know?)

Either way, I figured we needed all the help we could get. That's why I went to the chapel in the first place. I wasn't really sure what to ask for, or even how to start, so I just covered everything I could think of and hoped someone was listening.

It couldn't hurt, right? I mean, I wasn't ready to

be dead meat up in heaven or someplace much less desirable. Y'know, like dead meat on an open flame.

Okay, this is my prayer—"Rafe's Prayer."

"Dear God in Heaven…Is it okay to call you that? Anyway, it's me, Rafe. Khatchadorian. How's it going up there?

"Things aren't going too good down here. I was kind of hoping you could do something about it, if that's not too much to ask.

"I mean, I know you can do *anything*. But if you could watch out for me and my friends, I think we're going to need it. Another thing: I don't exactly understand why you had to create bullies. Of course, that's your call.

"And as long as we're talking, could you please take extra-special care of Mom and Grandma? And yeah, okay, my sister, Georgia, too. I guess. If you feel like it. She's not a bad person. Just annoying. Actually, I kind of like her. Don't tell anybody, especially Georgia.

"So, thanks for everything. Except maybe Doolin. And broccoli. I'm not sure what you were thinking there, but I guess you know what you're doing.

"By the way, I hope you can hear me. I don't really know how this works. I'm not even sure you speak English.

"*Habla español?* That's okay, me neither.

"Is this thing on?"

CHAPTER 51

GOING DOWN

By the time the sun came up, I was too tired to think straight and too wired to sleep. We agreed to stick together as much as possible that day, to watch each other's backs for whatever was coming, wherever it was coming from.

At breakfast, nothing happened. *Thank you, God, thank you so much.*

Nothing in school either. *Thank you, Ms. Kim. And thank you, God.*

Nothing at lunch. *Thank you, counselors. And God.*

In some ways, the waiting was worse than anything. It's not like we thought Doolin had forgotten about us. It was just a matter of time before the bombs started to hit.

Then that afternoon we had Day Two of the

Olympics. Surprise of surprises, the Muskrats came in dead last on the water-balloon slingshot. I did my best on the pole climb but got only halfway to the top. And we broke all of our stupid eggs by the second round in the stupid egg toss.

The whole time, all I could think was—

When's it coming? Where are the bombs? What's it going to feel like when I get hit?

Overhead, a huge crate (marked WATCH OUT BELOW!) hangs by a pulley on a rope, which is being burned through by a blowtorch. Buzzards are circling. Buzzard One: "It won't be long now." Buzzard Two: "I live for dead meat."

The final events of the day were the boating and swimming relays. Everybody was supposed to head down to the waterfront. I'm a pretty good swimmer, so I went to put on my suit. So did Smurf, Dweebs, and Cav. The rest of the guys went ahead with Rusty.

When I got there in my suit, everyone was standing around on the shore of Lake Wannamorra. Except Katie Kim. She was over on the dock, already soaking wet and looking concerned about something in the water.

"There's something very strange down there," she said. "I don't know what it is. But I can't move it by myself. It's too heavy."

Of course, about a dozen counselors and thirty or so campers started tripping over themselves to help her. The counselors ended up telling the kids to stay back for their own safety while Rusty and some of his brave cohorts dove down with Katie to get whatever weird thing was at the bottom of the lake.

After about ten totally tension-filled minutes, they managed to haul it up out of the water and onto the dock. Everyone watched. I mean, you couldn't take your eyes away.

"What the…?" Rusty said. "How did…? Who…? Why would…?"

It was a trunk! Someone had obviously thrown it in the lake, and now water was running out through the cracks and pouring all over the dock.

"It's locked up tight," Katie said. "Does anyone recognize this trunk? Or know how it got here? I want to know the truth!"

Oh man, oh man, oh man, oh man…

My stomach felt like it had just been ripped out, tied in a knot, and stuck back in my gut. Only it was way worse than that.

Yes, I recognized the trunk, all right. And I knew why it was so heavy. Because it was filled with all of Norman's precious books. So I guess the Bob-cats *had* heard everything after all. And they were willing to do anything and everything to get their revenge.

When I turned around to where he'd been half a second ago, Norman was long gone.

CHAPTER 52

MISSING IN ACTION

So, guess who's really good at disappearing? I mean like Houdini good. David Blaine good. Chocolate cake at Camp Wannamorra good.

Yeah, that's right. Starts with a Norman and ends with a...well, I never did learn Norman's last name. But you get the idea.

I told Katie whose trunk it was, and she told Rusty, who told Major Sherwood, who I'm pretty sure thought it was "all in fun" like everything else. They even kept going with the Olympics.

But after a while, it was obvious that Norman hadn't just gone off to the latrine. Rusty went up to the cabin to look for him, and when he came back, he said Norman's sleeping bag was gone.

That's when Major Sherwood finally started taking this seriously, and we all spent the rest of the day *not* finding Norman, all over camp.

We looked in the cabins. We looked in the tents. We looked in the woods. We looked in the latrines. Basically, you name it, and we looked in, on, under, around, behind, in front of, and between it. But still—no Norman. I'm telling you, that manhunt was strictly FBI. (I mean Fumbling, Bumbling, and Incompetent.)

After a while, even the girls' camp got into the game. Georgia came over with her new bestie, Christine, who wasn't anything like her brother, Doolin. When I told them what happened, they thought it was the worst thing ever.

"That poor kid," Christine said. "Which one is he?"

"Norman?" I said. "Skinny. Glasses. Reads like his life depends on it."

"Oh, Booger Eater," she said.

"THAT'S NOT HIS NAME!" I said.

I probably should have apologized for blowing my stack, but I had other things on my mind. Like for instance, how it was already getting dark, and Norman was nowhere in sight.

Then, just when it was looking desperate, Major
Sherwood got on the camp loudspeaker to make
things even worse.

ATTENTION, CAMPERS!
Please proceed to your cabins.
The search will continue
without you. Rest
assured, everything
is under control.
Except the parts that
aren't. Just kidding.
(Kind of...) Thank you
for your help, ladies
and gentlemen. NOW
GO TO BED!

I couldn't believe it. One of our own was still
out there, and they wanted us to scoot off to
beddy-bye? I mean, if a hundred people couldn't
find Norman, wasn't there a chance that Norman
was lost and couldn't find *us*?

Was anyone besides me even thinking about that?

I wasn't going to let poor Norman rot out there in the woods by himself. Especially after everything that had happened to him that day. And *especially* since this was partly (okay, mostly) my own fault. If I hadn't bulldozed Norman into being part of our whole revenge thing against the Bobcats, they never would have drowned his trunk in the first place.

So I did what Sherwood always said Camp Wannamorra men were supposed to do. I worked this one out for myself. While everyone else headed back to the cabins, I headed out to find Norman, once and for all.

Sayonara, Sherwood!

Have a nice night, everyone!

See you on the other side. I'm out of here!

CHAPTER 53

DON'T DO ANYTHING STUPID, RAFE!

Then, just when I was making my not-so-clean getaway, I heard a familiar voice behind me.

"*Ra-aafe?*" Georgia said. She was just about to get in her canoe with the other girls and head back. "What are you doing? I thought we were supposed to go to our cabins."

"We were," I said. "But I'm not."

"Isn't that against the rules?" she said.

This is one of the two dozen differences between me and my "beloved" sister. I've always thought rules were meant for breaking. At least the ones that don't make any sense.

On the other hand, Georgia never met a rule she didn't like. She lives for rules. She eats them for breakfast and dreams about them at night. No kidding.

"Wish me luck" was all I said to her.

"Luck!" she said. And then—"Wait!"

I turned around, and Georgia was running to catch up with me at the edge of the woods.

"Here, idiot. You might want this."

I looked down, and she was handing me her flashlight.

"Oh, right," I said. "Good call. Thanks." (She may be a rules zombie, but she's also a big thinker-aheader, unlike me.)

"And, Rafe, listen." Georgia got this serious expression on her face then. "There's something else you should know—"

"Georgia, let's go!" Katie Kim yelled from her little boat. "Rafe, you need to get back to your cabin!" She was looking at me like I was up to no good, so I didn't stick around for any more brother-sister bonding.

"I've got to go. I'll see you later," I said.

"Don't do anything stupid, Rafe!" Georgia yelled after me. "I mean, not any stupider than usual… which I guess leaves a lot of room for some pretty stupid stuff…but you know what I mean. DON'T DIE, OKAY? You hear me?"

I heard her, all right, but I was already headed off into the wild, black yonder. For better or worse. Smarter or dumber. Aliver or deader.

I wasn't giving up on Norman. I was going to find him if it took me all night.

And guess what? It kind of did.

SERIOUSLY,
WHAT WAS I THINKING?

Have you ever done something in your life that feels really good, like you're doing exactly the right thing...until, a little while later, when you're more like—

WHAT WAS I THINKING?

That was me about an hour later. I had been so gung ho, trying to figure out where Norman had gotten to, that I forgot to think about where *I'd* gotten to.

In other words, I was lost, lost, *lost* in the woods, like one of those socks that go into the laundry and never come back. (What's up with that, anyway?)

I was also feeling kind of stupid about the whole thing. Actually, a *lot* stupid. I figured Norman was probably back at camp by now, all tucked in for the night, and I was the one whose skeleton would be found after the spring thaw next year.

That's the thing about the woods at night. They're super dark. They're ultra-buggy. And when you don't know where you are, they're also scarier than a plateful of week-old mystery meat.

Sure, I had Georgia's flashlight, but all that showed me was the way to the next tree. And when you're lost in the dark, all those trees look alike. I guess I could have paid more attention on that nature hike, huh?

The only plan I could think of was to try to reach higher ground. I figured that might show me some lights from camp or any signs of civilization at all. So the first chance I got, I started heading uphill.

But it turns out that the woods around Camp Wannamorra are just as thick up high as they are down low. Plus, all that pitch-black was starting to play tricks with my mind. I was just wondering how many bites it might take for a bear to finish me off when, out of nowhere, I heard this voice coming from the dark.

And even that didn't make sense. It would have been one thing if the voice had said—

But it didn't say any of those things. This is what I heard instead:

CHAPTER 55

NOT SO ALONE

It was Norman, of course. But you probably already guessed that. I mean, if I hadn't made it out of the woods alive, I wouldn't be sitting here telling you this story.

Still, I shone my light in his face just to be 100 percent sure it wasn't the Wannamorra Strangler.

"WHERE HAVE YOU BEEN?" I asked. "Everyone's worried about you."

"Not everyone," he said. "Or else they wouldn't have let this happen."

I couldn't argue with that. Major Sherwood cared more about his tube socks than he did about us.

"Well, you're pretty good at hiding," I said. "It feels like I've been walking for a hundred miles. At least tell me you know the way back to camp from here."

"No problem," Norman said.

That was a relief. "Where are we, anyway?" I asked.

"Snake Hill." *Ohhh.*

"You can relax," Norman said. "There aren't any more snakes up here than anywhere else. It's just a name."

"How do you know that?" I said.

"I'm still alive, aren't I?" Norman said. I couldn't argue with that either.

"Anyway," he said, "we can go back, if you want. I'll bet even Major Sherwood's starting to worry by now."

"You know what?" I said. "Let him worry."

Sherwood had all these dumb camp rules, but nothing about keeping total maniacs from torturing other kids. I liked the idea of him sweating this one out. He was probably just starting to wonder what he'd tell Norman's parents when they came to get him at the end of the summer.

Meanwhile, it was a warm night. Norman already had his sleeping bag spread out. And best of all—

"Didn't you say something about sandwiches?" I asked him.

It turned out he had a whole loaf of bread, one of those giant jars of peanut butter from the Chow Pit, and a big jar of honey too. Sweet! As far as I was concerned, we were set for the night.

Really, there was just one thing missing.

CHAPTER 56

THE END IS NEAR

S o by the way, if you've been thinking...

Just hold on. Get your popcorn. Sit back and relax. Because it's all about to start.

This is what you might call the beginning of the end.

CHAPTER 57

UP AND AT 'EM

Here's the problem with sleeping while you're also breaking the rules: It goes by too fast. The next thing I knew, I was hearing that wake-up song from all the way down at camp. It was time for Norman and me to make some decisions.

Basically, we had three choices: We could stay put and switch over to tree bark and berries once the sandwiches were gone. We could hit the road in our tricked-out mobile home...if we had one. Or we could go back.

I told Norman it was his call. He said he was ready to face Major Sherwood, so we packed up his stuff and headed down Snake Hill.

"I think I made a huge mistake," he said while

we were walking. "Sherwood's going to send me home for sure."

"Don't worry. You're not going home," I said. "We'll tell him we got lost and had to wait for the sun to come up."

"That's not the part I'm worried about," Norman said.

I didn't know what he meant, but we were already coming into camp. I could see a whole bunch of people out in the main field. It looked like they were getting ready to start day two of the big manhunt.

But when we got closer, I saw that something else was going on. It was like there was some kind of giant checkerboard set up.

"What is that?" I asked.

Norman didn't say anything. He just got this big smile on his face. And then I saw why. It wasn't a bunch of white squares at all. It was about a hundred books, all lying out and drying in the sun.

"Hey, look who it is!" Georgia yelled out. She came running over and threw her arms around my neck like some kind of pet monkey.

"Okay, okay," I said. "You don't need to make a

whole thing about it. I know you were scared, but I'm fine."

"Don't flatter yourself," Georgia whispered in my ear. "I just need to tell you something. I was talking to Christine, and she knows what Doolin did. And *she* said—"

"RAFE! RAFE! RAFE! RAFE!"

All of a sudden, a bunch of other people were there, drowning her out. They were applauding and cheering and slapping me on the back like I'd just won the Indy 500 while blindfolded or something.

"Way to go, Rafe!" Tunz said.

"Didn't think you had it in you!" Cav said.

"I hope it was worth it, man," Bombardier said.

"RAFE! RAFE! RAFE! RAFE!"

None of this was making any sense. What was Georgia talking about? And what were the guys talking about?

"What's everyone talking about?" I asked Smurf.

He grabbed my arm and pulled me off to the side.

"We need to get you out of here," he shouted in my ear. "Sherwood's on the warpath looking for you."

"Just me?" I said.

"Yeah, like you don't know," he said. "When he went back to his cabin last night, it was totally trashed. There was peanut butter and honey all over EVERYTHING!"

"*Peanut butter?*" I said, looking over at Norman.

"And honey. Nice touch, by the way," Smurf said. "Sherwood got us all up in the middle of the night and started interrogating everyone. That's when he found out you were gone too. I mean, that's why you took off, right?"

I was still staring at Norman. I couldn't believe he had it in him. Because you can bet Sherwood would think it was "all in fun" when someone else's cabin got trashed. But when it was *his* place? Not so much.

Now I knew why Norman was afraid of getting sent home.

But I also knew I couldn't let that happen.

My head was still spinning when I realized everything had gone quiet. Nobody was clapping anymore. No more cheering. I hadn't had my back slapped in at least five seconds.

Then a big, round shadow fell over me. It was

like a meatball-shaped cloud moving in.

I felt a hand clamp down on my shoulder.

"Mr. Whatchamacallit," Sherwood said. "Do you have anything to say for yourself?"

This was it. Now or never. So I looked Sherwood in the eye, swallowed hard, and went for it.

"Yeah," I said. "You should tell Chef Rudy he's out of peanut butter."

FULL COURT PRESS

Within minutes, I'm arrested, fingerprinted,
cuffed, and dragged into the Dictator's court-
room for my trial. It doesn't take more than a quick
look around this place to realize—I'm not just in
a *little* trouble here. I'm in lots and lots (and lots)
of it.

"This court is now in session!" the judge booms
out. "Will the prosecution please call its first witness?"

"Your Honor, we call Rafe Whatchamacallit."

"Khatchadorian," I say.

"OVERRULED!" the judge says, and they drag
me over to the witness stand.

The prosecutor paces back and forth, licking his
chops. He's probably thinking about how I'm going

to taste after they fry me in the electric chair.

"Now, Mr. Khatcha-macallit—"

"Khatchadorian," I say.

"SILENCE!" the judge says.

"—where were you at the time of the crime? Exactly how guilty are you? And would you say you go better with rice, French fries, or baked potato?" the prosecutor asks.

He knows I've already confessed, so I've got to make this good. I'm fighting for my life here.

"Well, first of all," I say, "let me start by—"

"No further questions! That's all, Your Honor."

"But I didn't say anything!" I yelp.

"OVERRULED!" the judge screams. "Would the defense attorney like to ask any follow-up questions?"

Unfortunately, my "lawyer" is just a canoe paddle, so it doesn't have a whole lot to say.

"Next witness!" the judge says, and it only goes downhill from there.

Katie Kim says she saw me running away on the night in question. Rusty says he smelled peanut butter on my breath. Chef Rudy says I've stolen food in the past. Some kid from the Bald

Eagle's Nest thinks I just *look* guilty.

And then, before you can even say *mistrial*, it's all over. The judge pounds on the bench with his gavel and tells me to rise. He's ready to pronounce my sentence.

"After careful consideration of the evidence," he says, "not to mention *way* too much testimony from the suspect himself—"

"But I haven't said anything!" I say.

"QUIET!" he yells. "AND SIT DOWN!"

"You told me to rise."

"OVERRULED!" the judge screams. "Rafe Whatchamacallit, I hereby find you…"

CHAPTER 59

THE VERDICT

CHAPTER 60

GUILTY(iSH)

So yeah, I got the big boot, right out of Camp Wannamorra. But you already knew that, didn't you?

It all happened pretty fast. Right after I gave Major Sherwood my fake confession, he dragged me into the camp office and called Mom to tell her I was going to be checking out early.

That was it. I was heading home.

I guess the question right now is whether or not I need to explain myself to you. I mean, it's all right here in the story. But in case you missed something, here's how it added up in my head:

1 I started this whole thing.

OPERATION: SMOKE OUT THE BULLIES

+

2 Then I pushed Norman into it.

+

3 Norman already paid the price.

PROPERTY OF THE BOOGER EATER

+

4 He also had a really good reason for staying at camp.

GLUG GLUG GLUG GLUG

Bottom line? This one was on me.

I did it.

To be honest, I haven't spent a whole lot of my life doing things for people. Nice things. Good things. You know what I mean—all that stuff that makes you a "good person." And this seemed like a pretty good place to start.

I had my own stuff to deal with now too. *Bigtime.* This was about the eight million, six hundred forty-two thousand, nine hundred and ninety-ninth time I'd done something to disappoint Mom. She was probably going to kill me, and then kill my dead body, and then kill whatever was left of that.

Of course, the difference this time was that I hadn't actually done the thing I was in trouble for.

But let's face it. The chances of Mom believing *that* were somewhere around eight million, six hundred forty-two thousand, nine hundred and ninety-nine...

...to one.

CHAPTER 61

Dear Jeanne,

This is kind of weird. I'm sitting here waiting for my mom to come take me back to Hills Village (I'll explain later) and I'm just now getting around to writing you a letter. Who knows, you might even see my crazy face before you get this.

In fact, I hope you <u>do</u> see me first. Because that will mean I finally got up the nerve to do something I've wanted to do for a long time — ask you to go out with me. Like maybe to a movie. Or for pizza. Or a glass of water. (I'm not picky.)

I know it's kind of risky to write this before I even talk to you. Maybe I'll end up chickening out. Or maybe my mom won't let me out of the house for the rest of my life. (Again — I'll explain later.) Maybe you're even sitting there right now, reading this and thinking **WOW, WHAT A GIGANTIC L-O-S-E-R.**

But you know what? I don't care. And you know why? Because I think I'm kind of in love with you, Jeanne Galletta. So you might as well get used to it.

See you soon. (I hope.)

Rafe

CHAPTER 62

HOW MANY KINDS OF CRAZY DO YOU THINK I AM?

Nope. Didn't send that one either.
But who knows? Maybe one of these days.

CHAPTER 63

GEORGIA'S GOT A SECRET

Major Sherwood kept me in the camp office all morning, waiting for Mom and Grandma to get there. It was all kind of familiar. Hello, in-school suspension!

Or in-camp suspension, I guess. Same difference.

The only person who was allowed to see me was Georgia. She came in right before lunch. I figured she just wanted to say good-bye and call me a bonehead—which she did—but there was more.

"I've been *trying* to tell you something since yesterday," she said. "At least now, you can't run away."

"What are you talking about?" I said.

"Just listen, you bonehead."

Let's just say I wish I'd listened to Georgia a lot sooner. You'll see. Because this was big. *Huge.* A game changer, if I could pull it off.

But first, I had to deal with my other big problem. And in fact, I didn't know it yet, but she was just driving into the parking lot.

That's right. You know her as Jules Khatchadorian, mild-mannered waitress and all-around hard-working mother of two. But not today. Ladies and gentlemen, boys and girls, campers and counselors, please step aside (no, really—STEP ASIDE!) for the one...the only...the terrifyingly ticked-off...

WORLD'S! MADDEST! MOM!

CHAPTER 64

HELLO, NICE TO SEE YOU, PLEASE DON'T KILL ME

I didn't expect too many hugs when Mom and Grandma came in. And I got exactly one—from Grandma.

"What were you thinking, kiddo?" she said.

I guess she could afford to be a little nicer, since I hadn't spent half my life disappointing her. As for Mom, I'd say that on the Rafe Khatchadorian Scale of 0 to 10, we were somewhere between 0 and "grounded for life." I got one quick look when she came in, and she practically lasered me right out of my chair with her eyes.

Mom apologized to Sherwood a bunch of times. Then she told me to wait outside while they signed my release papers or figured out my torture-at-

home plan or whatever they had to do.

But I hadn't forgotten what *I* had to do either.

"Can I please go say good-bye to my friends?" I said. *"Please?"*

Mom looked at me, then at Major Sherwood, then at her watch.

"You've got fifteen minutes, Rafe. Not one second more. Then we're leaving," she said. Major Sherwood even gave me his stopwatch so I wouldn't have any excuse.

Fifteen minutes wasn't a lot. But at least I had a plan, thanks to my little sister. It turns out the kid has some game, after all. She was waiting for me behind a tree when I came outside.

"You know what to do?" I asked.

"All set," she said. "And Rafe? *Hurry.*"

"I will," I said, and kept moving. Because this was going to be super tight, and we both knew it.

CHAPTER 65

TICK-TICK-TICK

It took me less than a minute to run past the Chow Pit and make sure everyone was still at lunch. Everyone except for the Muskrats. Georgia had already gotten to them, and they were waiting for me up at the cabin.

When I came into the Muskrat Hut, all my stuff had already been packed and was gone. My bunk looked weirdly empty, but I didn't have time to worry about that.

The guys all stared at me like I'd just come from death row. Which I kind of had.

"What happened?" Dweebs said.

"Sherwood gave me the boot," I said. "I'm going home."

"What?" Norman said. "But...you can't. That's

not...you didn't—"

"Not now, Norman," I said. "I just need you to answer one question for me. Do you still have those big jars of peanut butter and honey?"

"Uh...well...yeah," he said. "Why?"

"Just get them."

You should have seen the way all the other guys looked at me—and then at Norman, when he pulled out those jars from his sleeping bag. It was like we'd just peeled back our faces and showed off the glowing alien heads inside.

But there was no time to explain.

"We've got to go—right now," I told them. "Smurf and Tunz, get as much poison ivy from behind the cabin as you can find. Bombardier, when was the last time you, uh...well, you know—"

"It's been a while," he said.

"Good. Come with me. Cav, Dweebs, Norman, you too. Smurf and Tunz, we'll see you there."

"*Where?*" Smurf asked.

"Bobcat Alley," I said. "While everyone's still at lunch." And before they could freak out too much, I

286

said, "Listen, I know what I'm doing. But nobody has to come if they don't want to."

That was it. Thirty seconds later, the Muskrat Hut was as empty as a kid's bed on Christmas morning. Tunz and Smurf were behind the cabin, picking poison ivy with socks on their hands. And the rest of us were headed up the path, straight toward Bobcat Alley.

Three minutes down.

Twelve to go.

Fingers crossed.

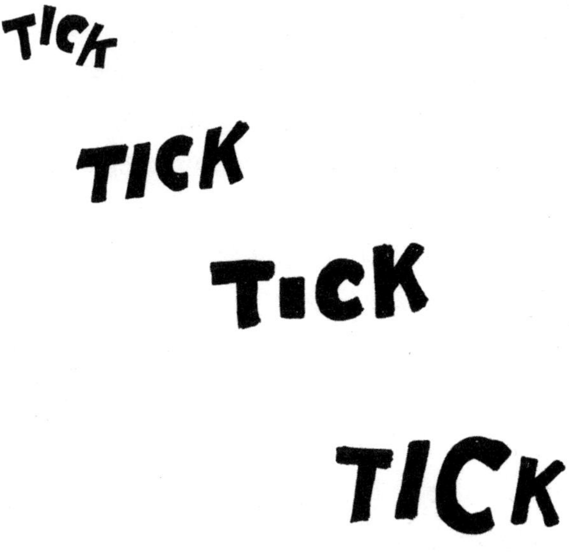

TICK

TICK

TICK

TICK

TICK

DON'T GET MAD, GET EVEN

All I could think about now was every wedgie, every stolen shoe, every shaving-cream balloon—every last, miserable prank Doolin and fiends had pulled on us since the first day of camp. This wasn't going to even the score exactly, but it was one giant step in the right direction.

When we got to the front of Bobcat Alley, I looked all the way down the field, where Georgia was waiting. I held up five fingers. She held up five fingers.

That meant five minutes before she was supposed to go over to the Chow Pit and "tattle" to Doolin about what we were doing up here. It wasn't much time, but you'd be surprised at what seven guys can do to one little cabin in five minutes.

Once we were inside, I went straight for Doolin's bunk. I pulled open his sleeping bag, stuck my hand in that jar of peanut butter, and started spreading it around like I was making the world's biggest sandwich.

Norman was right behind with the honey.

"Rafe, this isn't right," he said.

"Sure it is," I said. "The peanut butter always goes first."

"No. I mean, you going home. I don't know how to thank you."

"You can start by putting some of that honey in here," I said. So he did.

Meanwhile, Smurf and Tunz showed up and got busy with the poison ivy, all over the towels and washcloths. Bombardier was under the cabin, leaving behind a special surprise. Cav was gathering up all the shoes. Dweebs was taking the lightbulbs.

It was like we were all in a band, and everyone was playing a different instrument.

And the instruments were made of revenge.

Just like with anything awesome, it was all over way too soon. I was still putting peanut butter into

some dingus's sneakers when I heard the voices outside. They were far away at first but getting closer. *Fast.*

"What's for breakfast?"

"Dead meat!"

"What's for lunch?"

"Dead meat!"

"What's for dinner?"

"Dead meat, dead meat, DEAD MEAT!"

When I looked down at the stopwatch, it said I had six minutes and ten seconds left.

Doolin and fiends were right on schedule.

CHAPTER 67

THE LAST WORD
(STARTS WITH A *P*)

Oh, man!" Smurf said. He was looking out the screen door. "They've got baseball bats!"

"And sticks!" Cav said. "Lacrosse *and* hockey!"

They were pounding the ground as they came, getting closer by the second.

"Just stay calm," I said. "And stick close."

I went out the screen door first, with Smurf and all the other guys piling out behind me. Doolin was at the front of his pack too. We came face-to-face just at the bottom of the cabin steps.

"Loser up!" Doolin said, shouldering his bat. "You ever heard of strike four, Katch-a-cold? 'Cause I'm about to—"

"Come here, Doolin," I said, before he could get

any farther. (Believe me, I've learned a thing or two about Doolin's type. You've got to be as quick as they are strong.) "We need to talk. Right now."

"I don't feel like talking," Doolin said.

"But I insist," I said.

I don't think he was expecting that. He smiled, like I was entertaining him now. And then he followed me over, away from the other guys. Here went nothing. Or everything, I guess.

"I've got this sister here at camp," I told him.

"And I care about this *why*?" Doolin said.

"See, Georgia made friends with your sister—"

So it's like this....

"I'm yawning. See me yawning?" he said.

"And your sister told my sister about a nickname you had back in preschool," I said.

Doolin didn't say a word. So I kept going.

"I guess somebody used to wet his pants, Dools.

And this same person used to wear a certain paper product to school. And that *same* person used to be called Pampers. Stop me if you've heard this before."

It was like watching Doolin's face melt. By the time I got to the Pampers part, he looked about as happy as a Hawaiian snowman.

"What do you want?" he said.

"Less than you think," I told him. "You know Norman over there, right?" I pointed at the guys, who were standing off to the side. "From now on, that's his name. Not Booger. Not Eater. Not Booger Eater. It's *Norman*."

I took a step back now. Doolin still had that bat in his hand, and I liked my skull in one piece.

"You're joking, right?" he said.

"No joke," I said. "That's it. After this, I'm gone. You guys can prank each other all you want. Or not. I don't care."

Now he just looked confused, like he was still waiting for the punch line.

"But the whole Booger Eater thing is done," I told him. "That name's going into retirement. You got that, Pampers?"

"*Shh!* Shut up!" he said. "Yeah, yeah. Okay, fine."

"And I mean for everyone. Not just for you. Because my sister has a very big mouth. She won't have any problem telling every guy *and girl* at this camp about your nickname, if she has to."

I could tell we had a deal. And that was a good thing too, because the stopwatch was down to a minute and a half.

"So, how about you shake my hand while everyone's watching?" I said. "Tell them we made a truce. Then you never have to see my ugly face again."

I'm pretty sure Doolin was thinking about breaking my fingers while we shook—but I walked away fine. I took my guys back down the path, and he took his guys inside the cabin to start cleaning up. (If it were me, I would have started with what Bombardier left *under* the cabin.)

"What'd you say to him?" Smurf asked me while we were walking away. "What was that all about?"

"I just reasoned with him," I said. "Showed him the light, you know?"

"Yeah, right," Smurf said. He knew something was up, but there wasn't any time to talk about it.

My work here was done.

CHAPTER 68

SO LONG

I made it back with eight seconds to spare.

There wasn't even time to say a real good-bye to the guys, but I wouldn't have traded the way it went for anything.

Mom and Grandma were waiting for me when I got down to the parking lot. Georgia was there too, like nothing had happened. I gave her Major Sherwood's stopwatch.

"Tell the Dictator I said good-bye," I said.

"Let's go, Rafe," Mom said. "We've got a long drive ahead of us."

"So long, you big, fat loser," Georgia said. "See you at the end of the summer."

"Not if I smell you coming first," I said.

"Well, I see *that* hasn't changed," Mom said. But

when she turned her back, Georgia mouthed the words *good luck* to me. I gave her a thumbs-up and even a quick hug good-bye before I got in the car. Mom and Grandma never even noticed.

"See you, Georgia Peach," Mom said. "We'll be back to get you at the end of the summer."

"Drive safe!" Georgia said, and even stuck out her tongue at me to make it look good.

Then, just when we were pulling out of the parking lot in our ancient, wheezing, *maybe*-gonna-make-it-home minivan, Grandma pointed over to the side of the road.

"What the…?" she said.

That's when I saw the guys. They were all standing there, holding up a sign. Or six signs, I guess.

I turned around and waved while we drove away from Camp Wannamorra for good.

"I guess it just means they're my friends," I said.

That, and they still needed a new catchphrase.

CHAPTER 69

GROUNDED! DAY #1,332 AND COUNTING

So, no surprise, I'm pretty much grounded for the rest of the summer. Maybe when Georgia comes home, she can put in a good word for me.

But let me ask *you* something. Did I do the right

thing? Because I still don't know. Does getting into trouble make you a bad person?

Does getting into trouble for something you didn't do (because you want to help the person who *did* do it) make you a good person?

Does all this make your head hurt the way it does mine?

Anyway, it's not so bad. I've got Leo with me all the time now. I've got my sketch pad. And you might have noticed that I've been doing a little reading too. And by a little, I mean a whole, whole lot—for me.

Mom was pretty surprised when I asked her to get me that *Lord of the Rings* thing from the library—the one that Norman was so into. It's more than a thousand pages (!!!), but I'm giving it a shot. It's got elves and wizards and warriors from different places. It's basically good and evil duking it out with swords. Sort of like the different cabins at Camp Wannamorra. In fact, I like thinking about everyone I met this summer while I'm reading that story. And I probably wouldn't have even remembered the book, except for the letter I got from Norman about a week after I came home.

Hi Rafe,

I'm not really sure what you did, but everything's been different since you left. Well, not everything—but I think you know what I'm talking about. Nobody's even called me you-know-what in six days, eleven hours, and thirty-four minutes. (But who's counting?)

That's not even the biggest thing you did for me, though. And I think you know that too. If you ever need a favor, anytime, you should let me know. Maybe even next summer here at Camp Wannamorra. (I mean, if they let you back in. Which they probably won't.)

Anyway. I just wanted to say thanks. I'll always remember you, Rafe Whatchamacallit. And I've got a really good memory.

Your friend,
Norman

So that's pretty much it. Once I get out of this maximum-security bedroom of mine, I've got a few plans for the rest of the summer. Like, for instance, talking to Jeanne Galletta. I'm not going to tell her all that stuff I wrote in those letters. (Like I've said before—I'm crazy, not stupid.) But who knows? I just *might* get up enough nerve to ask if she'll go to a movie with me or something. Jeanne is cuckoo for those Hunger Games books, and there are some more of those movies coming out, I think. In fact... hmmm...maybe I should think about reading *them*. It might give us something to talk about.

But first, I'm going to finish the one I started. It's a pretty great read.

And, just like with my own story, I really want to know what's going to happen next.

P.S. MiDDLE SCHOOL IS ABOUT TO START AGAiN

So whether this was the best, worst, or in-between-est summer of my life, it has to end sometime. And you know what that means.

School is coming up again. (Boooo!) And my life isn't going to get any less complicated, that's for sure. I hear there's a new teacher at Airbrook Arts. Her name is Mrs. Stonecase, and supposedly she's the toughest nut *ever*. This lady won't crack, no matter what. They say she *does* the cracking, and I'm talking about skulls.

But then again, she hasn't met me yet, has she? So we'll just see about that.

CHAPTER 71

P.P.S.

One more thing:

Have you ever seen those shows where the narrator's like: "The names have been changed to protect the innocent"?

Same deal here. Except I'm also protecting the guilty.

Just so you know, Norman's name isn't really Norman. And Doolin's name isn't really Tommy Worley either. It's like that No-Hurt Rule of mine. (If you read my other books, you'll know what I'm talking about.) I don't think anyone, even Doolin, should have to go through life with a name like Pampers. Or Booger Eater.

At least, not because of me.

I guess the rest is up to them.

309

NOTE FROM THE AUTHOR

Dear Reader,

Bullying with words is more common than physical bullying, and sometimes it's just as damaging. And a lot more people do it—not just kids who are labeled "bullies." Even some teachers and parents can be word bullies.

So come on—stop word bullying! Nobody deserves to be called a "Booger Eater."

—James Patterson

High Adventure on the High Seas!

Turn the page for a sneak peek at
James Patterson's new series.

ON SALE **SEPTEMBER 2013**

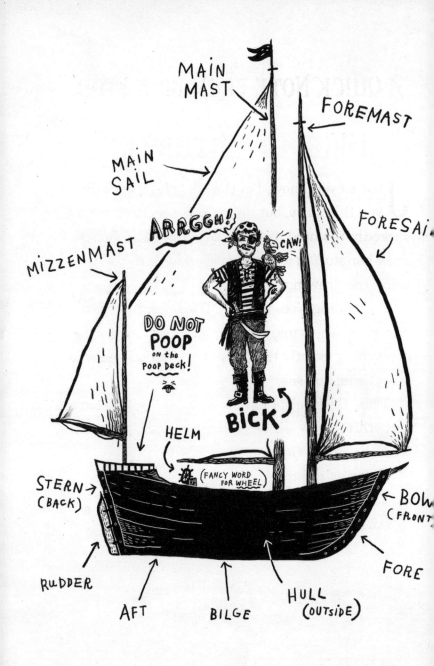

A QUICK NOTE FROM BICK KIDD

J ust so you know, I'm the one who'll be telling you this story, but my twin sister, Beck (who's wickedly talented and should go to art school or show her stuff in a museum or something), will be doing the drawings.

I'm telling you this up front because, even though we're twins, Beck and I don't always see everything exactly the same way. So don't believe everything you see.

Fine. Beck says I have to tell you not to believe everything I say, either. Whatever. Can we get on with the story? Good.

Hang on tight.

Things are about to get hairy.

And wet. Very, very wet.

1

L et me tell you about the last time I saw my dad.

We were up on deck, rigging our ship to ride out what looked like a perfect storm.

Well, it was perfect if you were the storm. Not so much if you were the people being tossed around the deck like wet gym socks in a washing machine.

We had just finished taking down and tying off the sails so we could run on bare poles.

"Lash off the wheel!" my dad barked to my big brother, Tailspin Tommy. "Steer her leeward and lock it down!"

"On it!"

Tommy yanked the wheel hard and pointed our bow downwind. He looped a bungee cord through the wheel's wooden spokes to keep us headed in that direction.

"Now get below, boys. Batten down the hatches. Help your sisters man the pumps."

Tommy grabbed hold of whatever he could to steady himself and made his way down into the deckhouse cabin.

Just then, a monster wave lurched over the starboard side of the ship and swept me off my feet. I slid across the slick deck like a hockey puck on ice. I might've gone overboard if my dad hadn't reached down and grabbed me a half second before I became shark bait.

"Time to head downstairs, Bick!" my dad shouted in the raging storm as rain slashed across his face.

"No!" I shouted back. "I want to stay up here and help you."

"You can help me more by staying alive and not

letting *The Lost* go under. Now hurry! Get below."

"B-b-but—"

"Go!"

He gave me a gentle shove to propel me up the tilting deck. When I reached the deckhouse, I grabbed onto a handhold and swung myself around and through the door. Tommy had already headed down to the engine room to help with the bilge pumps.

Suddenly, a giant sledgehammer of salt water slammed into our starboard side and sent the ship tipping wildly to the left. I heard wood creaking. We tilted over so far I fell against the wall while our port side slapped the churning sea.

We were going to capsize. I could tell.

But *The Lost* righted itself instead, the ship tossing and bucking like a very angry beached whale.

I found the floor and shoved the deckhouse hatch shut. I had to press my body up against it. Waves kept pounding against the door. The water definitely wanted me to let it in.

That wasn't going to happen. Not on my watch.

I cranked the door's latch to bolt it tight.

I would, of course, reopen the door the instant my dad finished doing whatever else needed to be done up on deck and made his way aft to the cabin. But, for now, I had to stop *The Lost* from taking on any more water.

If that was even possible.

The sea kept churning. *The Lost* kept lurching. The storm kept sloshing seawater through every crack and crevice it could find.

Me? I started panicking. Because I had a sinking feeling (as in "We're gonna sink!") that this could be the end.

I was about to be drowned at sea.

Is twelve years old too young to die?

Apparently, the Caribbean Sea didn't think so.

2

I waited and waited, but my dad never made it aft to the deckhouse cabin door.

Through the forward windows, I could see waves crashing across our bobbing bow. I could see the sky growing even darker. I could see a life preserver rip free from its rope and fly off the ship like a doughnut-shaped Frisbee.

But I couldn't see Dad.

I suddenly realized that my socks were soaked with the seawater that was slopping across the floor. And I was up on the main deck.

"Beck?" I cried out. "Tommy? Storm?"

My sisters and brother were all down in the lower cabins and equipment rooms, where the water was undoubtedly deeper.

They were trapped down there!

I dashed down the four steep steps into the hull quarters as quickly as I could. The water was up to my ankles, then my knees, then my thighs,

and, finally, my waist. You ever try to run across the shallow end of a swimming pool? That's what I was up against. But I had to find my family.

Well, what was left of it.

I trudged from door to door, frantically searching for my siblings.

They weren't in the engine room, the galley,

or my parents' cabin. I knew they couldn't be in The Room, because its solid steel door was locked tight and it was totally off-limits to all of us.

I slogged my way forward as the ship kept rocking and rolling from side to side. Whatever wasn't nailed down was thumping around inside the cupboards and cabinets. I heard cans of food banging into plastic dishes that were knocking over clinking coffee mugs.

I started pounding on the walls in the narrow corridor with both fists. The water was up to my chest.

"Hey, you guys? Tommy, Beck, Storm! Where are you?"

No answer.

Of course my brother and sisters probably couldn't hear me, because the tropical storm outside was screaming even louder than I was.

Suddenly, up ahead, a door burst open.

Tommy, who was seventeen and had the kind of bulging muscles you only get from crewing on a sailing ship your whole life, had just put his shoulder to the wood to bash it open.

"Where's Dad?" he shouted.

"I don't know!" I shouted back.

That's when Beck and my big sister, Storm, trudged out of the cabin that was now their water-logged bedroom. A pair of 3-D glasses was floating on the surface of the water. Beck plucked them up and put them on. She'd been wearing them ever since our mom disappeared.

"Was Dad on a safety line?" asked Storm, sounding as scared and worried as I felt.

All I could do was shake my head.

Beck looked at me, and even though her 3-D glasses were shading her eyes, I could tell she was thinking the same thing I was. We're twins. It happens.

In our hearts, we both knew that Dad was gone.

Because anything up on deck that hadn't been tied down had been washed overboard by now.

From the sad expressions on their faces, I knew Storm and Tommy had figured it out, too. Maybe they'd been looking out a porthole when that life preserver went flying by.

Shivering slightly, we all moved together to form a close circle and hug each other tight.

The four of us were the only family we had left.

Tommy, who'd been living on boats longer than any of us, started mumbling an old sailor's prayer:

"Though Death waits off the bow, we'll not answer to him now."

I hoped he was right.

But I had a funny feeling that Death might not take no for an answer.

READ MORE IN

ON SALE **SEPTEMBER 2013**